OctobeR

MidnighT

W.G. TUTTLE

October

Midnight

A Novel

THIS IS A
W.G. TUTTLE
BLURRED INK, LLC
BOOK PRODUCTION

Riveting fiction.

Novels

Those Who Long
Try To Sleep
October Midnight
War For The Spheres

Short Stories

Adamah - A Book of the Serpent
Scranton October 1894
SURvIVe
Cut-Up
Where Did THEY Come From?
Standard Issue Spirits
Vacation's End
A Fatal Thing

For my wife Shawn

Let them sleep undisturbed
Sealed and preserved
In their burial chamber

Once a year after Halloween night
They live once more through another's might
Inside a bodily container

Come midnight they awake
A soul for a soul to take
The souls in terrible danger

One soul will do if at least twice their age
But the unfortunate soul gets double their rage
Before returning to the chamber

1

Do I choose my life's path, or does fate decide for me? Abbie pondered, sitting on the couch in the living room, enveloped in her mother's arms.

"I'm so sorry, dear," her mother said, rubbing Abbie's back as she hugged her. "Losing someone is never easy, even when you know it's coming."

Abbie's dog, Oliver, had battled cancer for four months, spreading from the spleen throughout his body. Chemotherapy treatments had failed to penetrate the abnormal cells so stubborn and resistant that they may as well have been an alien lifeform surrounded by a force field that no one understood. A brief discussion of operating had ensued, but the veterinarian killed it quicker than cancer when he explained chances of survival were barely above the number zero. Small in other words—and so would be the dog—because much of his internals would have needed to be removed, leaving poor Oliver in an incomplete state and dependent beyond any living thing should be.

"I know, Mom. I just thought you couldn't do it. That you would wait."

"He was in pain, honey. Wouldn't you want to stop it?"

Abbie's moist face pressed into her mother's bosom. A muffled *"Yes!"* sounded when the sixteen-year-old girl finally answered.

A large exhale sprayed spit out of her mouth and snot out of her nose, wetting her face and the front of her mother's shirt. Thoughts first, then emotions, spread through her—like cancer—returning out of nowhere from some unknown place, remembering how cancer had killed her father two years ago. The thoughts and emotions weren't new. They were hers, for she recognized them, taking her back to that awful period in her life. Oh, how scared she was. What had scared her then had returned to scare her some more. *If I ever lose my mom?*

She knew Oliver had cancer and wasn't getting any younger, but never thought she would experience another death so soon. Too soon. Death piled on as if ready to take *her*.

The moody October wind outside pressed against the house, creaking what it could. Abbie's mother held her teenaged daughter tight, wanting her to feel her presence and love.

"I'm here, baby," her mother said.

Wrenching pain constricted Abbie's chest. *Don't leave me all alone, mom.* Memories of her father remained, but she sometimes forgot how life had been when he was around every day. And retaining those remnants seemed harder to recall each passing day. It made her afraid that, someday, she might not remember anything of her father.

Or Oliver, for that matter. Growing up with Ollie, she never knew life without him. At home, he followed her around, laid at her feet, her side, on her lap—always there. Sometimes, many times, the dog had faithfully been her best and only friend. She never minded.

Something she does mind: fate had intruded into her life twice and, when it had left, death had carried away two loves of her life—and there wasn't a damn thing she could have done about it.

2

The screen door slammed behind Abbie when she entered the kitchen through a side door. It took some force for Abbie to close the main door because the October wind whipsawed outside undecidedly as if it suffered from bipolar disorder.

"Hey, Abbie. How was school?" her mother asked.

Oliver used to greet me at the door, Abbie thought, then shrugged as she answered, "Okay, I guess."

"Dinner will be ready soon. *Oh*, before I forget." Her mom picked up a dishtowel, dried her hands, and picked up a small piece of paper off the counter. "I clipped this out of the paper for you."

A lingering hope inside Abbie moved her eyes, scanning the kitchen floor, in hopes of seeing Oliver.

Escaping the disappointment by reliving a better day, she remembered entering the house after school

4

and hearing the dog's nails tap the linoleum floor as he sped across the kitchen to greet her. Every time, he had entered a skid, colliding into her shins and feet to a stop, apparently, unable to learn his lesson. The excited, out-of-breath pooch chased its breath as her fingers scrubbed his head and behind the ears. The sensation of his soft coat between her fingers blurred the memory and reality.

The dog stood on its hind legs and reached its paws for her like a child wanting its mother. Its neck stretched toward her as its busy nose breathed in as much of her scent as it could. The dog's brown, alert eyes never left her face. Oliver was happy to see her.

How do I look to the dog? Abbie remembered thinking. *Does he know I'm happy to see him? Can he tell?*

"Abbie!" her mother interrupted, waving the ad. "I clipped this out of the paper for you."

When Oliver and the sensation disappeared, only bare linoleum floor remained. Depression welled up in Abbie. Annoyance, too, as she took the clipping so her mother couldn't wave it.

"What is it?" Abbie asked.

"Well, read it."

Turning it, Abbie saw it was a wanted ad.

```
Need a sitter for Halloween.
If interested call 717-171-7171
```

"Thanks, Mom," she said with a renewed countenance.

"Well, I thought maybe a little extra money would be nice, especially once you get your license. You're too old to trick-or-treat, so I thought it might interest you." Abbie's mom shrugged a shoulder. "You know—get your mind off things."

"I'll give them a call," Abbie said, exiting the

kitchen.

"After dinner," her mother's voice caught up. "Set the table, please."

Creaks followed Abbie's ascent up the stairs and, when she entered her bedroom, the heavy backpack thudded on the floor. A couple more steps, she plopped back-first onto her bed and it squeaked. Holding the ad above her, she reread it.

Need a sitter for Halloween.
If interested call 717-171-7171

Vague for an ad, she thought. *The area code is the same as mine, so it must be close. I'm sure once I call, whoever needs a sitter, will fill me in on the details. Hmm, only a two-digit number?*

Knowing she should get downstairs and set the table, Abbie sat up on her bed and placed the ad beside her bright red phone shaped like lips: the handset the upper lip resting on a bottom lip base.

As Abbie sat at the dining room table, eating, her feet and ankles felt naked. If Oliver were alive, his warm body would be covering them like furry slippers. Just thinking about it warmed her feet.

A familiar rattle sounded out of the kitchen. No doubt it came from the window above the sink. It always did—if the wind was strong enough. When Abbie was younger, it used to scare her. Still can, depending on the night and if she was alone in the house or not. It sounded too much like someone trying to get in.

Perhaps, the Holy Ghost peeked in through the window on the lookout for newborns before seeing blood smeared on the front and side door frames and passing over to the next house. Two blood streaks to be exact: her father's and Ollie's. That could be why it paused. If there had been a third, there was a good chance it would have kept moving.

What would have kept moving? A ghost, but not a *holy* ghost. God's protection wasn't over this house nor over those who lived in it. For how could anything dedicated to God search and destroy newborns? Or Abbie's father and Oliver for that matter? Why couldn't have death passed over?

In Abbie's memory, Oliver lived once more. Begging for food at the dinner table was never allowed. A smart dog, Oliver used to mind the rule. But once the family had gotten up from the table, begging had become fair game. Not eager enough to ask by barking, the dog, instead, used to prance around on its paws in anticipation of what scraps might land in his dish.

Abbie's memories fast-forwarded to a time when she remembered cleaning the dog dishes after Oliver's departure. The task came about because they needed cleaning rather than because of the death itself. Out of habit, the water and food dishes remained in their usual location, right alongside the refrigerator, instead of being put away.

Abbie's mom never said a word about the dishes staying out. In fact, Abbie had seen her mom pick up Oliver's belongings scattered throughout the house, wipe them off, and set them back down. It took a while for Abbie to catch onto this, but once she did, she realized her mother was also living inside a lingering, foggy denial. A fog so thick, it had caused Abbie not to see it until much later.

A chew toy, resembling a green zombie foot severed above the ankle with a bone sticking out of it, they had bought for Oliver last Halloween, still laid in the middle of the living room. Abbie remembered holding it by the bone, while Oliver gnawed and pulled on the foot in a game of tug-of-war.

There would be no prancing or tug-of-war tonight—the same as the last three nights. Only the October wind outside warred with itself as to whether it was coming or going.

3

Dinner all cleaned up, Abbie returned to her bedroom. After opening her backpack, it didn't take long before books, notebooks, writing and highlighting utensils, and calculator covered the rug. Before sprawling herself on the floor to start homework, she snatched her lips phone off her nightstand, plopped on her bed, sat for a second, before getting right back up to grab the ad she forgot.

A nervousness welled up inside her. Her eyes bounced back and forth between the phone number on the ad and the numbers on the receiver as she dialed. Each press of a button produced a kissing sound.

Hearing the other line ring, she became increasingly nervous. The handset, sandwiched between her ear and shoulder, steadied, now out of her shaking hand. The phone rang numerous times with no answer. After each unanswered ring, the nervousness she had felt dissipated.

Abbie looked at the clock on her wall, also designed as red lips, slightly separated, with black hands stemming out of the center of white teeth. The time was 7:05 p.m.

A couple more rings came and went without an answer, so she pulled the receiver from her ear to hang up.

The minute hand on her clock moved to 7:06 p.m.

Within the October wind, pressing hard against her bedroom window like an unashamed peeping perve, a faint *"Hello."* came out of the headset.

Hearing it, Abbie put the phone back up to her ear. *"Hello?* Is someone there?"

Untrusting eyes checked the window; the question for *it* as much as the person on the other end of the phone. *Is someone there?*

A sophisticated voice spoke through the phone. "Why yes, my dear. My name is Nora Thummel. And who might I be speaking with?"

"Abbie, ma'am. Abbie Syfert." Focused now, Abbie turned her eyes from the window as she continued. "I'm calling about the ad in the paper that you need a sitter for Halloween."

"Why, yes, dear. My husband and I placed that ad. We indeed need a sitter for this Friday. Are you interested?"

"Yes, ma'am. But I thought I could get some information first." *Since the ad was so vague.*

"Why sure. Of course, darling."

"Where do you live?"

"Station Knoll. 513 Spooky Nook Road to be exact."

"*Station Knoll?* That's forty-five minutes away. I thought you would be closer, having the same area code."

"Oh, dear," the woman said. "Just another learning experience for a young girl. You're how old, my darling?"

"Sixteen," Abbie answered.

"Oh, that's *perfect!* Just *perfect!* Growing up, but still a child."

"And how many children will I be watching?" Abbie asked.

"Two," the woman's voice crackled. "Two wonderful, perfect little children."

"And their ages, ma'am?"

"*Oh*, my two little angels. My handsome son, Kayne, is six, and so is my beautiful daughter, Kaleigh."

"It sounds like you love them a lot, ma'am."

"Oh, I do. I'd do anything for them."

"Well, ma'am, they would be safe with me. Now, as far as rates, I'm asking for $13 an hour with two kids and the drive. Speaking of hours, how many will I be watching them?"

"My husband, Hugh, and I will be attending a Halloween party. We don't get out much, so, say eight 'til eleven?"

"That'll be late with the drive home, so let me check with my mom."

"Dear, make sure to tell your mother we'll pick you up, take you home, and pay your going rate. *Okay?*"

"*Yeah! Okay!* Let me run it by my mom."

Abbie set the phone on the bed and trotted down the stairs to discuss it with her mother. They agreed to the arrangements, but Abbie must give her mother the address and their names, already having the phone

11

number from the ad.

"Okay, I'm back," Abbie said. "My mother said it's okay, but she would like to speak with you."

"Why sure, dear," Nora agreed. "A mother's trust is hard to earn when it comes to her children."

"Okay, here's my mom."

Abbie's mom talked with Nora, asking questions until she felt about as comfortable as she was going to talking on the phone. They arranged to meet this Friday, October 31, Halloween night, around seven.

Friday, October 31, Halloween Night

4

Friday came and the weekend was here. There was a home football game tonight and Abbie somewhat regretted she was going to miss it. It wasn't homecoming, senior night, or a rival game, so it wasn't a big deal, but she liked spending time with her friends. Besides, the money in her pocket next weekend would undoubtedly testify that tonight's sacrifice was worth it.

After taking her backpack up to her room, she raced downstairs and set the table for dinner. After, she helped her mother clean up and then started working on homework.

At 7:06 p.m., a black car pulled up along the front curb of Abbie's white, two-story, gable-front house situated on a hill among other similar homes. A woman got out, walked up to the front door, and rang the doorbell.

The hinges squeaked when Abbie's mother opened the door.

"Well, hello," Daphne said. "You must be Nora."

"That's right, and you must be Daphne."

Daphne motioned for her to enter. "Please, come in."

Nora looked around. "What a lovely home you have, Daphne."

"It's not much, but it'll do." Abbie's mom walked into the living room.

Despite wanting to get going, Nora followed.

Daphne motioned to the couch. "Please, have a seat."

Abbie came down the stairs and followed the voices to the living room. Entering, she stood beside her mother.

Daphne put an arm around Abbie. "Oh, good. I was just about to call you. Nora, this is my daughter, Abbie. Abbie, meet Mrs. Thummel."

Mrs. Thummel stood and shook the teenager's hand. "It's a pleasure to meet you."

"You, too." Abbie's mouth bent a little. "You sound a little different than when we spoke on the phone."

Mrs. Thummel placed her hand on her chest. "Oh, dear, do I? Phone connections can do that." She cleared her throat. "And I've had a little tingle. 'Tis the season."

"It's going around," Abbie's mom agreed.

Nora looked at her watch. "Oh, we better get going

14

if we're to be there by eight o'clock."

"Please." Abbie's mother motioned again toward the couch. "Just for a minute."

Nora looked around as she sat down. "Where's your dog?"

"How did you know we have a dog? *Had* a dog?" Daphne rolled her eyes.

Nora pointed. "The pull toy on the floor."

Embarrassed, Daphne picked it up. "*Oh*, that's Oliver's. *Was* Oliver's." She fought back the tears, wiping an eye. "He's gone."

"I'm so sorry for your loss."

"Thank you."

Daphne sat on the couch next to Nora and set Oliver's toy on the floor by her feet.

"I'm only going to say this once," Daphne started. "I have your names, address, and phone number. I know what you look like. We had a good conversation on the phone and you seem pleasant enough, but I don't know you from Eve. Everything better be on the up and up. Do we understand each other?"

"Absolutely, Daphne," Nora agreed. "I totally understand. She's your baby."

Abbie's mom wiped fresh tears from her eyes. "*Yeah—yeah*, she *is*. Always will be. She's all I have."

"No significant other?"

"*Yes*—and no. He's—"

"I'm sorry. I shouldn't have—"

"It's okay," Daphne said with emotion.

Unable to watch or else she would cry herself, Abbie turned away.

All three were in the same room, yet mentally couldn't be farther apart.

Nora checked her watch and stood. "We really

should be going or else we're going to be late for the party. As you can see, I still need to put on my costume."

Daphne stood, appreciating the change of topic. "Who are you going as?"

"Cleopatra and Hugh as King Tut."

"What a great idea," Daphne said. "Well, have fun."

She then turned to her daughter, wiping the occasional tear. "Got everything? Cell phone? Is it charged?"

"*Yep*. Ready to go," Abbie said.

Abbie's mom kissed her on the forehead. "Alright. Love you, baby."

"Love you, too, Mom."

Limply, Nora shook Daphne's hand. "It was a pleasure meeting you. We'll make sure to have her home by midnight. If we're running late, we'll call."

"Okay. Drive safe."

"We will." Leaning toward Daphne, Nora assuredly added, "And don't worry. I'm a mother, too."

An unsure smile formed on Daphne's face.

Aged hinges howled for an absent October wind as Daphne opened the front door and they all stepped out onto the porch. After another reassuring word that everything would be fine, Nora headed for the car. Daphne and Abbie hugged and exchanged words.

Abbie headed for the car, where Nora waited, holding the passenger car door open for her. The teen looked at her mother on the porch before getting in. Nora walked around the front of the car and got in the driver's side.

Abbie's mother stood on the porch, waving, as Nora turned the car around. Abbie waived back, blowing a kiss to her mother as they pulled away.

5

Mrs. Thummel checked her watch like clockwork, about every ten to fifteen minutes. Cruising in her 1984 Chrysler Fifth Avenue, she was making good time.

Abbie studied the car. "I've never been in a car like this before. It seems old, but nice."

"Yes," Mrs. Thummel agreed, bothered. "You could say the car is old when it's been around for over thirty years."

"Is it an antique?"

"*Oh*, I don't know. *Maybe.*"

More interested in the time, Nora rechecked her watch and saw it was a quarter 'til eight. "*Oh*, we're going to be late."

Abbie checked her cell phone for the time. Being late was one thing; trick-or-treat about to end another. Growing up, she had assumed donning a costume and going trick-or-treating was and would be part of life's ritual forever. Last year sure didn't seem like her last. Even when her mom had mentioned about sitting instead of trick-or-treating, it never registered. Until now, nearing eight o'clock, the register dinged and opened up a whole new world—without trick-or-treat.

As they entered a small town, a worn wooden sign greeted them, "The neighborhood of Station Knoll welcomes you."

Mrs. Thummel reduced her speed.

Decorated for Halloween, homes and businesses, on both sides of the street, charmingly testified October neared its end. Almost every porch, doorway, and step had at least one pumpkin and many of them had small hay bales or other decorations, making the town festive for fall.

Carved or painted pumpkins, used as heads, topped hay-filled dummies, sitting on benches and rocking chairs. Dry corn stalks wrapped many light poles and porch posts. Nowadays, stringing lights were popular and everywhere, mostly orange and purple, but people also used their Christmas lights of green and red, appropriate for the season.

Yards adorned with zombies, ghouls, and the demonic captured autumn, many of which contained sensors that triggered movement and sounds out of them when passed by. Small figures in well-lit areas looked like the decorations they were—nothing scary about them, appropriate for future and young trick-or-treaters.

But, oh, those life-sized mannequins in dark places! Not only were they *life-sized*, but every year, these things appeared more *life-like*. Name nearly any masked or deformed killer and it was like meeting them in person. And when the damned look-alikes were placed ominously behind trees, hedges, and fences in a stalking manner, best be advised to stay away. Who knew whether they were decorations or the real deal?

Best to be on the lookout, too. Why foolishly wander into them like an unaware character in a horror movie? No one wants to stumble upon these things, but if it happens, remember to look frightened as hell when confronted with the evil. A high-pitched scream never hurt, if you have the lungs for it, followed by a deep moan, the kind when battling constipation on the toilet, to suggest how intense and gut-wrenching such an encounter would be. Because one never knows—the cameras may be rolling.

Skeletons, corpses, and sheet ghosts hung from trees; sporadic wind gusts swept through, rattling their bones and breathing life into them. Fences aligned with Halloween-themed garland divided most yards and the sidewalk. Several homes had fake cobwebs spread around their covered porches and some all over the front of the house.

Corn-kernelled tough-nuts went as far as boarding up their windows. And we're not talking about homes a step above condemnation either. No, some homeowners living in houses a step below a mansion had boards nailed over their windows.

The extent to which the street was decorated surprised Abbie. Compared to her neighborhood, the main drag of Station Knoll looked more like a movie set than a real town.

In her neck of the woods, only one house could compete with these houses on Main Street, Station Knoll without being embarrassed. Decoration-wise that is, not the house itself.

Every year, without fail, the owners of this lone-standing Satan-lair went all out, displaying their collection of horror galore. Each year they added something new to their exhibition, which covered the front of the house, the entire front yard, including the tree, and now extended into the driveway. Maybe they were trying to make up for everybody else, but the house stood alone as the *scary house* of the neighborhood. Unlike Station Knoll, which had several *scary houses* on its main street alone.

"They really decorate for Halloween around here, don't they, Mrs. Thummel?" Abbie asked.

"Celebrating and decorating for Halloween has grown in popularity, but for decades it's been my family's favorite."

At a snail's pace, Mrs. Thummel drove through town, watching for trick-or-treaters moving up and down both sidewalks and crossing the street at will.

October's wind blew a plastic facemask out of a young boy's hand, over the curb, and into the street. Of course, the trick-or-treater followed. If Mrs. Thummel hadn't been driving slow and carefully watching, she surely would have hit the little Teenage Mutant Ninja Turtle.

"Whoa, Mrs. Thummel!" Abbie said. "These kids aren't watching, are they?"

"No, they're not. Nor who is supposed to be watching them."

"Good thing you're going slow."

"Well, let's just say I have an invested interest."

"You care about them," Abbie said, not confirming nor asking.

"Aren't these kids taught the purpose of the mask?"

Mrs. Thummel went on. "It's for their own protection, so they aren't recognized. It wouldn't have blown into the street if the kid had the mask over his face."

Abbie's forehead wrinkled as she asked, "What do you mean?" For she had never learned about the origin of Halloween, the Celts, Druids, or the ancient festival of Samhain.

"They don't teach kids anything in school anymore. Just keep your eyes peeled."

And with that, Mrs. Thummel drove on.

6

A few minutes after eight o'clock, Abbie noticed trick-or-treat continued and thought, *Lights would have been out before the hour on my street, guaranteed.*

Now, not all of the lights stayed on in Station Knoll, prolonging the festivities. A good number of them had been turned off promptly at eight. Town's folk, who had passed out candy from their porches, had had enough, dousing their lights and quickly gathering their things to get inside a warm house.

Right on! That's what Abbie was used to seeing. Technically speaking, eight o'clock ended trick-or-treat. Sure, fair enough. Rules are rules and were meant to be lived by—these party-poopers would agree. The party started at six and ended at eight. At which time, the music abruptly stopped mid-song, everyone kicked out of the place, and the lights turned off. Six to eight—no more, no less. No disputing that.

Unless you were a rebel and believed rules were made to be broken by keeping the lights on and letting the music play, knowing trick-or-treat would breathe its last breath soon enough. Why usher in death when it would naturally occur on its own? Rebels had the wisdom to see this, where impatient party-poopers were quick to stab repeatedly trick-or-treat to ensure it died, as it took its final breaths. Cold-blooded. But there aren't many rebels now, are there?

Still, a scattering of outside lights—rebel lights— remained lit, letting trick-or-treaters know they were still open for tricks-or-treats. There were only a few houses where human candy dispensers still sat bundled outside, braving trick-or-treat's dying breaths, occasionally blowing through the town, while most rebels did their rebelling inside a warm house, still willing to answer the door when called upon.

Knowing this *grace period* wouldn't last long, costumed kids scrambled door-to-door to get what they could before lights went out. Last call, as it were. A number of front doors were open, as smiling distributors passed out candy, trying to get rid of what they had left.

It was kind of exciting to watch, not knowing when lights would turn off, letting everyone know they were done partying for the night.

At some point, lights would be turned back on to resume their regular duties of lighting the area near the front door.

Until next year, when trick-or-treat night sneaks up from behind and yells, "Boo!" How deliciously exciting to be caught off-guard by a night as sweet as trick-or-treat night? A time when off-the-hook children possess animal instincts and can smell sugar so thick in October's air, they can taste those freebies like little vampires detecting blood flowing through veins. Turned on, indeed!

Not a bad gig at all. A little bit of walking, or running, door-to-door and the greedy consumers receive a year's worth of candy in two hours. Of course, it was eaten in mere weeks, days, or hours if not monitored. But why save it? Thanksgiving was coming. Then Christmas. And New Year's and Valentine's and Easter. Goodies had to be eaten. Fruits and vegetables gone bad could be tossed out with the rest of the trash. Who needs them? But toss anything out with sugar in it—even when it was free—Satan forbid!

Which, of course, it wasn't free. Few things are. Parents bought candy for other children only to be returned through other parent's purchases given to their children. A give and take no different than any stock exchange or trading post.

And don't feel bad for those grandparents. It was common knowledge grandparents at all levels of grandness bought candy *they* liked, willing to pass out most of it in exchange for not feeling guilty they had purchased the goodies for themselves. Still, these experienced tricksters monitored inventories closer than gold bars at Fort Knox, ensuring a stash remained for when they were in the mood for a treat.

Not all candy carried the same value on this exchange, but kids who hit enough homes usually brought more candy home than what their parents had spent for trick-or-treaters. If anything, the candy exchange had simplified over the years. Handing out fruit or novelty trinkets, such as oversized pennies, had been delisted from trading on the exchange some time ago.

Fruits and vegetables—who needs them? What's a trinket? Can't spend an oversized penny.

A young boy, wearing his midget football uniform for a costume, set a bulging pillowcase full of candy on the sidewalk, picked up a rock, and threw it at the closest street sign. The rock pinged the metal just as Abbie read it from inside the Chrysler Fifth Avenue passing by.

Abbie couldn't believe he threw it. It wouldn't have hit the car or gone into the road, but people were walking the sidewalk. Not many, but all it took was one mishap and the midget jock would receive a penalty much worse than any enforced on the football field.

Up ahead, a marker, pointing to a park, looked familiar to Abbie. Closer now, she recognized it.

"I played softball there," Abbie said, pointing. "I wondered if we would pass this place. That's how I knew how far Station Knoll was away from my house."

Mrs. Thummel's eyes moved from the road to her side mirror, back to the road, to the rearview mirror, and returned to the road. "You know where you are?"

"Kind of. I don't think I could get home on my own from here if that's what you mean."

"That's what I mean."

"Especially in the dark. Guess I'll have to get better with directions when I get my permit."

"Well," Mrs. Thummel checked her watch, "nothing to worry about."

Abbie studied Mrs. Thummel. *Where's the* dear *or* darling? *I don't think she said either since getting in the car.*

She turned away from the woman and looked out the passenger side window, recalling how Mrs. Thummel had said she had a *'tingle'—'Tis the season.'* The woman's voice on the phone compared to the one in person didn't jive.

Approaching the town's edge, Station Knoll abruptly ended with an old train station up ahead on the right. In passing, the train stop was still in service. Lights were on and a few people waited for the next train. Beyond the station, nothing but harvested fields. Darkness replaced what had grown on them, blending in with the night sky.

The car's headlights shined on the upcoming road sign for Spooky Nook.

Mrs. Thummel drove by.

"Hey, Mrs. Thummel!" Abbie exclaimed. "I thought you said you lived on Spooky Nook Road."

"We do, dear." Mrs. Thummel said, her eyes checking her mirrors. "I always go down one more road, then circle back. It's closer to where we live."

Oh. Now she says, 'dear.'

The car's blinker sounded and at the next right, Mrs. Thummel turned.

A discreetly released sigh unwound Abbie.

Unsteady headlights revealed a badly cracked paved road with chunks missing, flanked on both sides by harvested cornfields. The wind picked up and, being in flat, open land, a gust of October's wind pressed against the passenger's side of the car, strong enough to sway the cabin on its wheels. The blinker flashed brightly in rhythm with the tick-tock sound as Mrs. Thummel made another right. Abbie noticed the road sign missing from the post.

They crossed the railroad tracks, went a little farther, turned left, then another left onto a well-compacted, smooth dirt road, crossing the railroad tracks again. Night and none of the roadways marked disorientated

Abbie.

Abbie's cell phone awakened, casting a light on her face. Seeing it was twelve past eight, Abbie asked, "Are we almost there?"

"Oh, yes, thank goodness," Mrs. Thummel said and sighed as if she had walked it instead of drove it. "It's just ahead."

"Sorry for making you late."

"Oh, it's alright. We're in good shape."

As Abbie strained to see, she turned and happened to notice her own reflection in the passenger door window. Distorted by the glass with the night behind it, her face appeared older. *'Too old to trick-or-treat,'* her mother had said.

Emerging out of the cornfields off the dirt road to a clearing, the ride of the car felt different, rolling on a partially-paved surface. Ahead, tucked amid a cluster of trees, was a house, its frame barely visible within them. Other than a couple of lighted windows on the first floor, the rest of the house appeared dark.

"Is that your house?" Abbie asked.

"The back of it, yes." Relief flashed momentarily on Mrs. Thummel's face, only to be replaced by worry.

A wave of windblown leaves scurried across the backyard. A small barn sat to the left of the house.

"Do you get any trick-or-treaters out here?" Abbie asked.

"No, dear. Not a one. We're too far away from everyone."

Abbie twisted at her waist in the seat, looking around. In every direction, there were sporadic white and yellow lights of other homes, but nothing close. The train station lights were barely visible and the town behind it not at all.

"Is this still Spooky Nook Road?" Abbie asked.

"Sure is."

A dinging sound from the direction of the train station caught Abbie's ear, so she turned in her seat and looked out the back passenger window behind Mrs. Thummel. High-pitched squeals cried through the night air from a train braking.

Abbie turned toward Mrs. Thummel. "That's loud."

"Eight-fourteen on the button." Mrs. Thummel didn't have to look at her watch. "Six trains a day, dear."

Abbie straightened in her seat and faced forward again. "When's the next one?"

"Ten-forty-eight. I have my own built-in alarm clock, telling me it's time to go to bed."

"Doesn't it wake the kids?"

"*Oh, no.* The kids are *very* deep sleepers. They're out like a light by then."

Pulling up to the back of the house, Mrs. Thummel noticed Hugh's silhouette in the back door window, his hand holding back one of the curtains. Hurriedly, she parked the car and said to Abbie, "Let's go."

7

As they got out of the car, a strong gust of October air pressed against their bodies like wind against sails, stopping their forward progress for a moment, then giving up and letting them proceed.

Mr. Thummel opened the back door, flashed a smile at Abbie as she entered, then stopped smiling as his wife came in. Some leaves blew in, tumbling and sliding on the linoleum kitchen floor before he closed the door.

"*Man* is it windy out there tonight!" he said.

Mrs. Thummel marched through the kitchen and straight down the hallway through the center of the house to go upstairs to change into her costume.

Abbie didn't notice it entering the house, perhaps the open door and wind had masked it, but the distinct smell of old people percolated in the air like stale coffee—from a century ago. The familiar, musty air reminded her of her grandparents' house and, admittedly, her grandparents, whose perishing bodies emitted a festering decay which overpowered any room, especially when they were together. No amount of perfume or cologne could mask the smell of death. How could it? With death embodied inside and seeping out of their pores, the truth of dying since birth lingered underneath, for Abbie always smelled it. And she didn't have to be close. Their cooling bodies warmed death's funk enough to distribute its potpourri throughout any room.

Looking at Mr. Thummel, she thought, *The Thummels can't be any older than their late thirties, early forties.* Then she considered, *Maybe it's from the previous owners.*

Feeling something on her head, Abbie swiped a hand over her hair. A gold-colored leaf, turned but not brittle, tumbled down the side of her head to her shoulder, then down the front of her chest where she caught it. Holding the leaf, she looked up.

Mr. Thummel's dark-gray pinstriped suit, black tie, hair, and mustache contrasted against the all-white kitchen. The chain attached to his lapel, down to the pocket watch inside the breast pocket of his double-breasted suit coat, swung as he shyly approached the sitter. His hesitation came off awkward, as if he hadn't been next to a stranger in a long time, perhaps not trusting himself.

When he stopped at Abbie's side, no more than an inch away from her, his cheap cologne mixed with the mustiness in the kitchen and reminded Abbie of her grandfather.

Mr. Thummel's chest rose and fell as he breathed, either labored or excited. His face moved in close and, when his nose touched Abbie's hair, his eyes closed and he breathed in, smelling the young girl.

Uncomfortable and creeped out, Abbie stepped back, giving herself some space.

Mr. Thummel's demeanor changed, appearing both confused and pissed off that she had moved away from him. This state sent mixed signals to his body. Hesitantly, yet impatiently, he stepped within an inch of her again, his black dress shoes cracking on the linoleum floor.

"I'll take that," he said.

Fear tingled Abbie's spine. Instead of paralyzing her there, it made her flee, albeit not far, as she backed up a step.

Flustered, yet determined, the man followed, as if dancing in-step with a partner.

Immediately, she continued back another pace and, this time, he remained a step away.

The extra space allowed her to see him holding out his hand, flat and palm-up, with his elbow tucked at his side as if amid a karate movement.

Confused fear contorted her face. A tickle in her hand made her realize perhaps he spoke of the leaf— *'I'll take that'*—and not her.

Abbie reached to place the leaf in his open hand, but before she could, he moved it, touching the top of her head and pressing her hair against the side of her face, caressing it.

"My daughter has beautiful auburn hair ... just like yours," he said.

Holding the leaf, Abbie wanted to move, wanted to flee, but paralysis had already begun. Hounding her was one thing. Smelling her was another, enough to close every pore in her skin in suffocation. Touching her reached inside, constricting everything under the skin, a protective shutting down. All within the first few minutes of walking through the door.

Repeatedly, his hand stroked her hair like a brush on a horse.

Abbie's eyes glossed over, proof her insides were congealing.

Finishing a stroke, Mr. Thummel stopped, brought his hand close to his face, and stared at it. Then, through his spread fingers, he saw the sitter's face, numbed beyond expression, yet, beneath the glaze over her eyes, her irises screamed with fear like little mouths, and he awakened out of his infatuation.

"Oh!" he whispered. *"Oh, dear! I'm so sorry. I didn't mean…"*

"Didn't mean what?"

Mrs. Thummel stood in the kitchen door by the hallway, wearing a long suede black dress with an exposed V-neck pointing down between her breasts, long sleeves ending in points over the back of her hands, and formfitting material flattering her curves at the waist. Straight, long, black shiny hair covered her shoulders and reached her bosom. Lying flat against her pale chest was a pewter necklace with a garnet-colored stone.

Gulping, closing his eyes, and then reopening them, Mr. Thummel said to Abbie, "Here, I'll throw that away."

Cautiously, Abbie placed the leaf in his hand.

He took it over to the trashcan and threw it away, while the rest of the leaves that had blown into the house lie scattered on the kitchen floor.

Mr. Thummel's black pinstriped suit and Mrs. Thummel's black dress confused Abbie.

"I thought you guys were going as Cleopatra and King Tut?" she asked.

Mr. Thummel turned around, his demeanor different as if nothing had happened.

"Every year we dress up as Gomez and Morticia Addams from the Addams Family," he explained. "You could say it's a tradition."

Mrs. Thummel's eyes locked onto Hugh's as she leaned back against the refrigerator with her arms flat against it. A bare knee appeared through the slit in her dress as she placed the bottom of her dress shoe against the refrigerator door. Standing on one leg, she asked with an accent, "Gomez, my darling. How do I look?"

Staring, Mr. Thummel got into character. "To die for."

Playfully, Mrs. Thummel's face turned away from him, her eyes locking onto Abbie, as she said, "One can only hope."

Mr. Thummel's black dress shoes shuffled across the kitchen floor as he moved toward Mrs. Thummel. Grabbing her hand, he pulled it away from the refrigerator, straightened her arm, and kissed the length of it.

"Say something in French," he said between kisses.

Fluently, she granted his request. *"Lécher ma chatte."*

"Comme un serpent," he said, equally fluent.

Kissing and groping one another, the Thummels made out against the fridge, ignoring the sitter.

Not sure what she got herself into, Abbie wanted to undo it.

"Uh, hum!" Abbie sounded.

It took a couple of interruptions to get the Thummels' attention to stop.

33

"It's almost a quarter 'til nine," Abbie added.

"Yes, we should be going, my love." Mr. Thummel's hand raised with his index finger pointing at the ceiling. *"But,"* he accentuated, "I got you something."

Acting shy, as if he shouldn't have gotten her a gift, he left the kitchen, went into a joining room, and returned, holding something behind his back; his face molded in a cheesy grin.

"Oh, Gomez," Mrs. Thummel said, surprised. "You always did know how to build the suspense."

Out from behind his back, a single black rose appeared. "A rose for my thorn on Halloween. Do you like it?"

"I loathe it," she said, accepting it. "Just one little touch will make it perfect."

She carried the rose over to the kitchen counter, laid it on the chopping block, grabbed a knife, and hacked down on it. Holding up the stem, she said, *"There.* I abhor it more."

Black rose petals covered the cutting board.

Mr. Thummel came up behind her and caressed her curves with his hands. "Nothing says Halloween like a good decapitation." With a sudden gusto out of character, he said in his usual voice, *"Whelp,* let's go."

Abbie's eyes scanned the hallway while her ears listened intently. *"Wait!"* she said. "Aren't you guys forgetting something?"

Mr. Thummel's head shook side-to-side. *"Nope.* I think we got everything we need." His opened mouth headed for Mrs. Thummel's exposed neck.

Before he got a nibble, Mrs. Thummel turned around, smacked his shoulder to stop, and said, "The *children.*"

"The *children*," Mrs. Thummel repeated. "They're upstairs in their rooms."

Abbie shrugged. "For six-year-olds, they're awfully quiet."

"Why, they're sleeping, dear. It's almost nine o'clock."

Geez! I let some of my inexperience show, Abbie thought, then asked, "In case of an emergency, how do I get in touch with you?"

"Yes. You're a good sitter," Mrs. Thummel said as she walked over to the kitchen table. "All the information is right here."

A sheet of paper laid on the table. It looked old and worn as if written years ago, maybe decades.

"Is that a cell number?" Abbie asked.

"No," Mrs. Thummel answered. "We don't own cell

phones. Our house is right smack in the middle of a dead zone. That's the number to the house where we'll be."

Abbie pulled the cell phone out of her back pocket. It had plenty of battery, just no bars.

Mr. Thummel touched Mrs. Thummel's elbow. "Honey, we should go. It's almost nine and we have a half-an-hour drive yet."

As the Thummels headed for the back door, Abbie wanted them to leave, saying, "Have a good night. I'm going upstairs to meet the kids."

Mrs. Thummel's voice sounded encouraging. "Yes, you do that. Spend some time and get to know them."

Mr. Thummel grabbed a black shawl off the coat rack in the corner between the back door and kitchen table and placed it around Mrs. Thummel's shoulders.

Mrs. Thummel's thin arms crossed over her chest and her long bony hands caressed the shawl, as she looked at Abbie and said,

"Let them sleep undisturbed
Sealed and preserved
In their burial chamber
Once a year after Halloween night
They live once more through another's might
Inside a bodily container
Come midnight they awake
A soul for a soul to take
The souls in terrible danger
One soul will do if at least twice their age
But the unfortunate soul gets double their rage
Before returning to the chamber."

Abbie gulped. "Did you write that?"

"No," Mrs. Thummel answered, speaking as she returned to the kitchen table. "It wouldn't be right of me to take credit for something I didn't write."

Her long fingers lifted the paper with the phone number. Underneath laid a small piece of paper with writing on it.

"Would you mind reading this to the children after we leave?"

Abbie stepped closer to look at it. The paper looked in about the same condition as the paper with the contact number on it, worn and aged.

"What is it?"

"A poem, my dear."

"I thought you said they were sleeping."

A slanted smirk appeared on Mrs. Thummel's face. "Probably not yet. I may have been a little hasty saying they're asleep when my husband just put them down before we arrived."

They're going to send me home if I keep screwing up, not knowing things, Abbie thought, then apologized. "I'm sorry, Mrs. Thummel. My mistake. I'll read the poem."

"Nice and loud, so they hear, *okay?*"

"Okay."

A soul-grabbing stare by Mrs. Thummel suggested it had better be okay. If it had been a staring contest, Abbie would have lost within the first seconds.

"She'll do nicely," Mrs. Thummel said to Hugh, then demanded, *"Let's go!"*

The Thummels headed for the back door.

Abbie followed a couple of steps before stopping near the center of the kitchen.

"Have fun," she said but didn't mean.

"Oh, we will," Mrs. Thummel said, not bothering to turn around as she exited the house as Hugh followed, closing the door behind them.

Once they were out, Abbie walked, then trotted

over to the door and locked it. Opening the curtain with a finger, just enough to peek out, she watched them get into the car and drive away.

9

Abbie leaned against the back door and exhaled. *Okay. A quiet house. The kids are down. And only two hours to go. Piece of cake.* Then she wondered, *Will I still get paid for what we agreed to or, since it's nine o'clock, will they deduct an hour?*

Grabbing the poem off the kitchen table, she headed down the hall and went upstairs. Standing on the landing, she examined her surroundings. *All of the doors were open, except these two.* Continuing down the hall, she stretched her neck, peeking inside each open room. *Bathroom. Master bedroom. Sitting room.*

Backtracking down the hall, she returned to the two closed doors. *These have to be the kids' rooms.* Her hand surrounded one of the doorknobs and tried turning it, but it was locked. So was the other knob. *What? How am I supposed to care for them if the doors are locked?*

Nothing was going right. Frustration, *no*—beyond that, way past that, sometime in the past before Halloween existed and at some point in the future when Halloween itself was history because no one celebrated it anymore.

This night was evil. As a youngster, dressing up in costumes and trick-or-treating for candy, she never saw its wickedness. Spanning over a decade of going door-to-door for, let's face it, *treats*, because no one wanted to perform *tricks* anymore on other people's kids because they'd get sued, have their name smeared, and their bank account pillaged. Not once was she forced into a house, touched inappropriately, offered alcohol or drugs, found a razor blade or anything else inside an apple other than its core, or anything to suggest Halloween was evil.

Older now and experiencing tonight—she saw it—and felt it, being touched by Mister. This night does things to people. It changes them. She didn't know how or why, but it does. Maybe the Thummels were weird year-around. Probably a safe bet. Either way, the Thummels were off. This sitting gig was off. And so was this Halloween night.

After staring at one door, then the other, unsure what to do, she leaned a shoulder against the left door. Those same feelings surfaced and quickly turned to anger. Her shoulder pressed against the door while she wiggled the knob. Gradually, the slope of her lean shallowed as she put her weight into it, just in case the door was stuck or jammed.

It didn't budge.

A lean became short thrusts of her throwing a shoulder against the door. Then, the other door. Until pain warmed the inside of her shoulder and she stopped.

This wasn't the way. This was dumb. Halloween was changing her and she felt stupid for allowing it to happen.

You're better than that, Abbie thought. *Think this through.*

Climbing on a ledge or ladder or something outside to get to their windows weren't options because there was no way she was doing that. The risk itself didn't warrant it, but, *oh*, that wind.

Yelling for the kids to open the door was a possibility, but what if they're asleep? Maybe letting them be was best. Yes, perhaps it was.

Still, the locked doors puzzled her. *Why would parents lock the doors? Don't they trust me? Maybe? But then why hire me? Mr. Thummel was the one who put the kids down for the night. Perhaps it was an accident? He didn't know they were locked. And the kids locking themselves in didn't make any sense unless it happened accidentally.*

Odd. The whole thing as peculiar as the parents. The puzzle seemed unsolvable.

Unless—unless the kids had locked the doors to protect themselves.

Maybe, but I'm only the sitter. That's all. Whatever's going on here is none of my business. I don't want to know.

And there it was. Abbie had convinced herself. Besides, what harm could happen to the kids sleeping in their rooms? Likely none. Perhaps, dealing with the parents had been the hard part.

A sense of relief washed over her when she realized she didn't have to solve it. All she had to do was be in the house with the tikes a few more hours and she would be out of there, certain she wouldn't be back.

She could do that. Cruise on easy street for a bit, get

paid, get home, and tomorrow turn onto nearly any store street she wanted—within reason—nothing like the shops on Rodeo Drive in Beverly Hills, California.

After all of that, Abbie was back to yelling through doors. It was a tough call. Both rooms were quiet; the kids were probably asleep. So, instead of yelling through the doors, she settled on talking.

With her mouth an inch away from the door, she called, "Kayne? Kaleigh?"

Not hearing anything, she stepped in front of the other door. "Kayne? Kaleigh? You awake?"

Silence.

"If so, open the door, okay."

Nothing.

"You should only lock your door when a stranger is in the house. I mean, I'm a stranger, but a good stranger, here to watch you. So, even though I'm a stranger, you should keep your door unlocked so I can get to you in case of an emergency."

No response. After that hodgepodge, she couldn't blame them.

"Well, okay. I'm supposed to read you this poem, so I'm just going to read it."

Lifting the poem so she could see the words, she read it nice and loud.

"Let them sleep undisturbed
Sealed and preserved
In their burial chamber
Once a year after Halloween night
They live once more through another's might
Inside a bodily container
Come midnight they awake
A soul for a soul to take
The souls in terrible danger

One soul will do if at least twice their age
But the unfortunate soul gets double their rage
Before returning to the chamber."

God, that's morbid! Abbie thought. *What a weird poem to read to six-year-olds. But, whatever.*

"Okay," she yelled into the rooms. "I read the stupid poem and your doors are locked, so I'm going downstairs now."

As she stood there, listening, no sound came from behind the doors.

"You know what, fine," she said and headed downstairs.

10

With the poem on the kitchen table next to the contact number, Abbie debated with herself whether she should call the Thummels about the kids' doors being locked. Part of her didn't want to come across inexperienced, but knowing the doors were locked and not calling, probably showed more inexperience, especially if an emergency happened and she had to get the kids out of the house. The only way now entailed breaking down the doors. Which she questioned she could do after her shoulder's bout with the door and her shoulder lost.

Abbie picked up the contact number off the kitchen table and carried it over to the phone, hanging on the wall. After dialing the number, the phone on the other end began to ring, then increasing tones pierced her ear as an intercept message in a recorded computerized imitation of a woman's voice said, *"We're sorry; you have reached a number that has been disconnected or is no longer in service. If you feel…"*

Abbie hung up and pulled her cell phone out of her back pocket. No service. Mrs. Thummel had said earlier that the house sat smack in the middle of a dead zone.

Dead zone. Sounded about as safe as eating a cafeteria lunch. And not just the school's, but any cafeteria.

Returning to the wall phone, she tried redialing the number, only to get the same intercept message. Defeated, she hung up.

What a disaster! No cell service. Wrong number. I have nothing to tell the operator. I can't contact the Thummels. I'm in the middle of nowhere, in some dead *zone, far from home. It's like I'm sitting for the real Addams family. Gomez and Morticia are out having fun, while Pugsley and Wednesday are presumably locked in their rooms.*

Worry filled her.

I hope nothing goes wrong. Maybe it already has. I wouldn't know because the doors are locked. I hope they don't blame me for anything. They're *the kids' parents. They* should have *childproofed the doors so they couldn't be locked from the inside.*

Do I call mom?

Using the landline, it was an option.

From a teenager's perspective, trying to be responsible, it wasn't. She wanted to handle this on her own. The situation hadn't changed. Everyone was okay and accounted for.

Damn her mind! How did she know? She didn't know. Not for certain.

I'm where I'm supposed to be and marginally okay, but what about everyone else? The kids may or may not be in their rooms.

They may be okay; they may not be. The Thummels might be at the party, or maybe they decided to do something else—like make out. I could call home, but it doesn't mean mom's there to answer.

She laid the contact number on the kitchen table and moseyed down the hall to find a TV. *If they have a TV.* Mindless watching might trick her into quit thinking about this night and mentally escape to someplace else.

As she peeked into the room on her left, the foyer light, near the front door, shed enough in for her to see it was a formal living room—without a TV.

Checking the room to the right, she didn't see much. The foyer light only penetrated enough of the room to expose a landing. A couple of steps beyond that, darkness.

As she stepped onto the landing, her eyes searched for a light switch. As they did, they saw two silhouettes, standing at the back of the room in front of a white-curtained bay window lit by an eave light outside.

All of her instincts said to run, but her legs tightened with that heavy, tingling feeling that happens when you haven't moved a body part for a long time. *Sleep,* they call it.

Simultaneous screams and pleas came out of her innermost being: *STAY AWAY FROM ME! GET OUT! DON'T HURT ME! DON'T HURT THEM!*

If she were a betting girl, she would have bet tonight's sitting fee that she had screamed those words aloud. But, fitting this Halloween night, she would have lost, because they had never crossed her lips to leave the body to make a sound.

With her legs anchored to the landing like end posts on a handrail, deadened limbs standing in a dead zone, she wasn't getting the betting slip to the bookie in time, anyway. Good thing, because tonight's trouble would have netted nothing. At this point, the pay was still in play.

As far as the other two in the room, it was hard for her to tell whether they were moving or not. The visibility wasn't exactly ideal. In fact, it was getting worse.

One moved.

Tricks on the eyes were no treat. Maybe it wasn't a trick.

A twitch sparked in her head, shot down the spinal cord to her waist, darted back up her spine, and slammed into her brain. Nearly simultaneous as if in cahoots, a vibration rattled her heart, ran spiraling laps around her spinal cord, down then up, before colliding into her heart. The crisscross sensations were too much for her body and she collapsed on the landing.

Through blurred vision, the silhouettes in front of the bay window appeared to move toward her. It was the last thing she saw before blacking out.

11

Outside, a high-pitched squeal windsurfed October's breath through the night into the Thummel house. Abbie's stiff, sore body began to move as she came to. The slits of her eyes struggled to open because the lights in the room were on.

How are they …? Mentally formulating the question hurt her head too much to finish.

The squealing sound continued like a relentless alarm. Not only to wake her up but alarming her something was wrong.

Her eyes eventually widened, accepting the light. Getting to her feet, Abbie paused, waiting for her equilibrium to balance. When she slid her cell phone out of her back pocket, the time said it was 10:52 p.m.

I've been out for over an hour!

Again, the words, merely thought, stung her brain as

if each one made a fresh cut when thought. It was hard for her to imagine what the pain would have been like if she had spoken them.

Her mental capacities awakened and it occurred to her the squealing sound was the ten-forty-eight train at the station, just as Mrs. Thummel had said driving in.

There was still no cell service, so she returned the phone to her pocket. In a dead zone, it seemed foolish for her to check, perhaps a little insane, expecting to see service, but she couldn't help it, she had to check, and maybe that alone made her a little mad. At least the phone kept time and that in itself maintained some order.

Using the wall as a handrail, she went down the steps into what must be a recessed family room. Overly decorated for Halloween, it could pass as a display in a store.

"Kayne! Kaleigh!" Abbie yelled. Speaking wasn't as bad as she had thought, so she said some more. "Did you turn on the lights? It's okay. Come on out. Let me see you."

Keeping her distance, she examined what had scared her. Two life-sized props were positioned in front of the bay window: one a naked man, the other a naked woman. Both weren't fully developed, missing faces, hair, holes, and sex organs; mere bone and flesh structures completely covered in skin. The only giveaway they were a man and a woman was their build: the man taller and more muscular, and the woman had nipple-less breast bumps on her chest.

As she proceeded closer toward the props, they moved, the man bending slightly forward while raising his arms out chest-high like a zombie—Abbie thought to grab her—and the woman's head, which had been positioned somewhat to the left, turned to face forward—Abbie thought at her. The damned things moving like that made Abbie squeal like the train coming into the station.

Suddenly, her squeal stopped, turned off by the lack of air—her own—because she now held her breath. Out of the man prop's mouthless face muffled, *"Help me."*

No, help me! Abbie thought and it hurt—those cuts again.

Somehow, someway, she faced the woman in time to witness a terrified woman's face appear through the skinned-over face of the prop in the form of a video, as if the woman were trapped inside her own body, begging, *"Let me out!"*

No, let me out!

Some freaks with a backassward appearance or they had done something ass-backward had a way of trickling into those hard to reach places of a person and scrub up deep-welled laughter—much like a drain cleaner loosening grime. Not these freaks. These barebacked, bare-assed, animated stiffs scared the bejesus out of her. She can honestly say that she had never seen anything like them before. Why the hell the Thummels had them in their home was beyond her.

In a struggle to turn from them, she finally looked away for a moment—only a moment—then back at them. Trust came hard, as hard as the pliable rubber coating their framed, yet life-like bodies. So far, the dummies hadn't moved or spoken another word since.

Now, believing the props were through giving her any grief as long as she kept her distance not to trigger any movement or words, Abbie moved on.

When she had looked away for that moment, her

eyes saw what she had sought over an hour ago. A big-screen TV sat on a stand with glass doors. Occasionally peeking over her shoulder at the skinned abnormals, she moved toward the TV. An extensive library of horror movies, stowed away in the cabinet, could be seen through the glass. Most of the titles she had never heard of before.

Watching TV had lost its lure and there was no way she was watching a horror flick, not after experiencing tonight's horror. All she wanted now was out of the room, out of the house, and as far away from the Thummels as she could.

Starting that process, she climbed the steps onto the landing. *Who turned on the lights?* She had nearly forgotten—and walked into the foyer, thinking, *I'm glad the Thummels didn't come home while I was out.*

No, that wouldn't have been good. The only thing Abbie had watched so far was the back of her own eyelids. It occurred to her that she might never set an eye on the kids she was hired to watch.

The desire to phone home welled up like a full bladder. At sixteen, she still wanted her mom—needed her. Not calling, as if deciding to hold it and pee later, at some point, she would have to go. Still groggy, she moseyed down the hall, ready for the night to be over. But first, she had to pee.

12

As Abbie became more awake and aware, time bogged down, sluggish, as if sleepy. The poem and bogus contact number laid on the kitchen table in front of her as she sat and waited. *After I'm paid and safely home, I'm going to ask, What's up with the number? On second thought, no I'm not—I'll be home.*

Bored, she re-read the poem silently to herself. None of it made sense and she was too out-of-sorts to try to figure it out.

So her mind switched to the kids. Probably because they were the ones she was to read the poem. And let the record show, she had read it to them. Through doors, *'nice and loud'* as Mrs. Thummel had suggested. *'So they hear, okay?'*

'Okay,' Abbie had said.

But it wasn't okay. There were no images for them.

Nearly impossible when the whole concept of sitting was to watch, in a caring fashion, children who could not care for themselves. There were supposedly two six-year-olds in the house—in their bedrooms—but who knew for sure.

Her mind created images of them. Kayne appeared as a spitting image of Mr. Thummel: pale skin, dark hair, and dressed like Gomez Addams, only dwarfed. Kaleigh was a mini-clone of Mrs. Thummel: pale, jet-black hair, and dressed like Morticia Addams. The images as disturbing as the naked backassward freaks in the family room.

Abbie thought, *Maybe I should check on them before they get home.*

Sliding the kitchen chair out from the table, she ventured down the hall. The light in the family room was still on and she went upstairs. Not knowing who had turned on the lights had rotated her stomach up to her heart, her heart up to her brain, and her brain down to her stomach. Of course, there was confusion, her mind down there. Who could think straight with their internals jiggered like that?

In checking both doors, they were still locked. An inkling the rooms may be empty resurfaced, this time with fear. *Why would they bring me out here to watch two children that don't exist, while they go to a Halloween party?*

Halloween? Abbie remembered Mrs. Thummel saying, '*...for decades it's* (Halloween) *been my family's favorite.*' Roaming spirits! She had said it driving through Station Knoll, right before avoiding a tiny trick-or-treater wearing a Teenage Mutant Ninja Turtle costume. Trick, indeed! *How could I be so stupid to miss something so obvious?* Abbie wondered. *If Halloween's a family fave, then why weren't the kids out trick-or-treating?*

Abbie's heart beat faster than the seconds keeping time. Terrible thoughts flashed one right after another in her mind—Halloween thoughts on Halloween night.

Abbie backed away from the doors, unaware she was doing it. She shuffled down the stairs, through the hall, and into the kitchen. Antsy, she paced the kitchen floor. *They should be here any minute.*

Eleven o'clock came and went. Eleven-o-five. Eleven-ten.

Maybe Mr. Thummel had taken the kids trick-or-treating for the first hour or so and came back early to get ready for the party? Abbie reasoned. And reasonable it was.

Eleven-fifteen and the Thummels still weren't home.

Abbie wrestled with calling home. *They're only fifteen minutes late.* Paralyzed in her indecision, time continued past eleven-thirty. *They're only thirty minutes late.*

Her pursed lips popped as air moved through them and then they flattened into a straight line across her face. *It could be serious. Maybe they got in a car accident or something.*

Indecision moved her into pacing. First toward the phone, away, then toward it again. This time, she picked up the receiver. Her thumbs punched in her home number as if typing a text message. When she placed the receiver to her ear, there wasn't a dial tone.

Confused fear grew into anger. Tempted to bang the handset against the housing, she thought the better of it, instead, staring at the phone, as if it could understand her expression before hanging it up.

Her heart pounded in her chest. It was crazy for her to check her cell phone and, sure enough, there still wasn't any service.

Not knowing what to do made her crazy. Indecision

had her on the move again, this time toward the back door. She found herself stepping toward it, away, then toward it again as if dancing with it. Finally, she opened the door.

"AAH, GEEZ!" she yelled.

Mr. Thummel stood outside the door. Behind him, a lady Abbie didn't recognize.

"Going somewhere?" Mr. Thummel said as he entered the house, forcing Abbie back into the kitchen. The lady followed and, as she walked in, an entourage of fall leaves blew in around and under her booted feet like a rolled-out orange carpet.

Long, pitch-black hair encased her head, looking like a hood attached to the black dress she wore. A silver chain, around her neck, contrasted against the black fabric of her dress, as did the silver oval, which appeared empty but wasn't, holding a black pendant, which blended in against the black dress. Only the pale skin of her face and hands were visible. Rare red eyes, not a deep red, but pale, made the woman appear the only way red eyes would make anyone look—evil.

Abbie backed farther away. "You're not the same woman. Where's Nora?"

The lady closed the door behind her.

Before it closed, Abbie's professionalism went out into the October wind, her face scowling at Mr. Thummel as she said, "Where were you? You were supposed to be here at eleven to get me home by midnight."

Mr. Thummel played coy. "Oh … that … well."

The lady pushed Mr. Thummel aside, replacing him where he had stood in front of Abbie. "Don't mind him, dear."

Everything widened on Abbie's elongated face. "*It*

was you! You're the one I spoke with on the phone."

The woman ran a finger through the side of Abbie's hair, looking at her as a cherishing mother would.

Abbie pushed her hand away and stepped back. "Don't touch me! Where's Nora?"

The lady smiled. "Why, I'm Nora, dear." Then, her smile disappeared.

"*No! No!* You aren't the same woman that picked me up, drove me here, and that he was groping on earlier."

Nora Thummel, the real Mrs. Thummel, turned and shot Mister a look that she would deal with him later, undoubtedly, distributing nothing but pain.

Not saying a word, afraid to speak, he only pleadingly gestured as if to say, *I wasn't groping on her— she's lying.*

"That was my sister, Noreen, darling," the real Nora said, glaring at her husband. "At this hour, she's probably sleeping on a plane—or with another man."

Head jerking, Nora's crazed, red eyes snapped to the sitter.

Abbie didn't like that look. Full of intensity and intent to harm.

"But most likely sleeping," the woman continued. "Just as you were, dear, about an hour ago."

Abbie's nervous mind raced, repeating the same lap. *They were watching me.*

"What?" Abbie intoned.

A fake laugh slipped out of Mrs. Thummel as if at a cocktail party. The sudden mood swing made Abbie flinch. About as unpredictable as the Earth exploding and, in the blink of an eye, nothing remained.

Lighthearted amusement never jived with red eyes.

"You know, darling," Nora said. "The nap you took

on the family room landing."

13

A car passed in front of Abbie's home; its sound and lights at that hour, the last hour of Halloween, were enough to have Abbie's mother look out the window. *Eleven-forty-five. They're cutting it close, aren't they?*

She stood by the front door for the next fifteen minutes, looking out the window and listening for the phone.

It was almost midnight and still no word.

14

Approaching midnight, Mrs. Thummel explained to Abbie why her sister, Noreen, was the one who had to pick her up and meet her mother. If she had shown up with her pale skin and red eyes looking like a possessed albino, would Abbie's mother have agreed to let her go? Would Abbie have wanted to go? Of course not. No time would be good.

Sorry. All I have is midnight right before bed this coming Friday, the 13th—oh, I'm sorry, a little dyslexia there—I meant the 31st—yes, that's the one. But me not being able to see you and you being able to see me with those infrared eyes, well, that just won't do.

No, it wouldn't. Not on Halloween night of all nights.

While Mrs. Thummel explained, Abbie cried the kind of cry of someone defeated, soft and subtle with the damnest of hurts in her heart, as Mr. Thummel bound her hands and feet to one of the kitchen chairs with rope, rustling leaves on the kitchen floor as he worked. Red splotches on Abbie's face stung from Mrs. Thummel slapping her every time she had interrupted her story with wimpy moans. And the tears on her cheeks didn't help. Instead of being a soothing ointment, they aggravated the stinging.

Still, they didn't hurt like the defeatism killing her will inside. This night had already put a good beating on her. Beyond strange and nearly incomprehensible how emotions and circumstances could hurt worse than physical pain. But, often they do. As unforgettable and unforgivable this night had been, the agony of defeat, ruthless and destructive, had already started spreading roots in Abbie's mind, heart, and spirit, taking hold like long, ugly tentacles on a monstrous hand. Digging them out was the only way of getting rid of them before being destroyed from the inside-out like spontaneous combustion. And there was no way around losing some of the mind, heart, and spirit along with it.

Mrs. Thummel paced in front of Abbie as if giving a lecture, explaining how Noreen had always been the nice one, having a successful "agreement" rate, as she liked to call it, of getting kids to come to the house. Unlike her own, her sister's face went well with any hair color or style, attractive as a blonde, brunette, or redhead. Sure there was always a risk of being recognized, but not every job entailed her meeting parents or any adults for that matter. Sometimes, many times, Noreen coaxed the kids directly. Besides, the money was good, starting her vacation to get out of town for a while. Do the deed, satisfy the greed, and recede to the rear for a little R & R.

Like a teacher in a classroom, Mrs. Thummel stopped and asked Abbie if she had any questions.

Through tears, Abbie asked, "How did you know I passed out on the landing?"

Missus pursed her lips and answered, "Hugh drove Noreen to the train station, dear, where her car was parked. At some point, he paid her a large sum of money in cash. I'm sure she and my husband swapped spit before she got in her car and drove to the airport. See, dear, she was already packed and ready to go with her bags in the car. Taking a different route, Hugh drove back to the house and, with the lights off, parked behind the barn. We met in the barn and walked up to the house to watch you through the windows. We saw how worked up you had gotten, darling, seeing the mannequins and collapsing to the floor."

"So *you* turned on the lights," Abbie said. "Why didn't you wake me?"

"We checked you and you were fine. My goodness, we'd thought you'd sleep it off, but you're cranky."

"Why me?" Abbie's head hung. "Why is this happening?"

"*Why?* Because you called, my dear. You wanted the job and now you have it."

Mr. Thummel started a countdown. "Six minutes 'til midnight."

Abbie looked up at Mrs. Thummel. "The kids aren't real, are they?"

An expression contorted Missus' face. "They are. As real as you or I."

"Where are they, then?" Abbie asked.

"Why in their rooms, darling, just like I told you earlier. You've known all along, haven't you?"

Mister's voice escalated. "Five minutes 'til midnight."

"Why the poem?" Abbie asked. "Why read it?"

There was that look again on Missus' face. Abbie didn't like that look.

"You're assuming they didn't hear you," Missus interpreted. "*Oh*, they heard you, dear—as you'll find out soon enough. Every sitter learns the truth of the poem as it unfolds."

Excited, Mister could hardly contain himself, pointing a long index finger vehemently into the air. "Four minutes 'til midnight!"

An emotion-filled exhale blurted out of Abbie worse than when she had cried over Oliver's death in her mother's arms. Through hysterics, huffing, and puffing, she asked, "What … happens … at … midnight? … Am I … going … to die?"

Bending over, placing her hands on her knees, Mrs. Thummel stared at the teenager; her white face and red eyes protruded in Abbie's tear-blurred vision.

"Midnight," Missus said, "is when the real Halloween party begins."

"But…Halloween…will be…over."

The nose on Missus' face wrinkled as it went arrogantly into the air. *Stupid girl*, Missus thought. *Schools and religious groups don't teach these damn kids anything anymore.*

"Halloween, darling, is the beginning of Allhallowtide, which used to last three days, but like most things had been contracted down to two. *Today*, on Halloween, we remember our loved ones no longer with us and the gap between the living and the dead narrows, allowing the dead to crossover with us. *Tomorrow and the next day*, on All Hallows' Day and All

Souls' Day, we remember and honor the dead with our lives."

"Three minutes to midnight!" Mister announced.

Her pride deflating, lowering her nose, Mrs. Thummel continued her lecture.

"Come October midnight, when October ends and November begins, the gap between the living and the dead is at its thinnest and most crossovers occur. The dead cross for many reasons. Some good. Some bad. But they that learn of the portal come. A party of invited—and uninvited guests."

Stressful emotion had rubbed Abbie's throat raw. A scratched squeal started her sentence, making her voice unrecognizable. "*Wh...wh...why* are you telling me all of this?"

Mrs. Thummel straightened, looking down at Abbie tied to the chair. Arrogance raised her nose; then, she lowered it. Holding back her excitement, she casually said, "Because, my dear, the story dies with you."

15

"Two minutes to midnight!" Mister announced.

With crazed red eyes, Mrs. Thummel raised her hand as if making a proclamation. *"Cut her loose!"*

Mr. Thummel walked over to the kitchen counter and pulled a knife out of the block set. Slowly he turned and, holding the knife out in front of him, approached Abbie.

The sight of a pale creep dressed in a suit from the 1930s, holding a knife and coming toward her, slipped Abbie's mind into a dream-like state. Fog blotted out the kitchen. Psychedelically, Gomez's form warped as if going back in time to the 1960s when the sitcom aired. This couldn't be happening. A show. An elaborate Halloween prank. An adult, Mr. Thummel surely had to know this was wrong, didn't he?

But, *oh*, that knife. It *was* real. As real as the

overhead lights reflecting off what metallic parts remained of an otherwise tarnished blade. For some reason, the weapon was uninhibited by the fog or warping, its boundary clear and crisp, the blade's cutting edge sharp.

Did Mrs. Thummel say, 'Cut her?' Abbie couldn't remember. *He's coming at me like he's going to cut me.*

With that knife, now within an inch of the young girl's face. So close, Abbie saw her reflection in it, fragmented, parts clear in the sheen, others dull—psychedelic, a metallic tie-dye. It made her appear older—just as the passenger window in the car had on the way to the house. And it wasn't groovy.

Neither was the blade backing up like a coiling snake and slashing in a downward arc across her face. Instinctively, Abbie quaked.

Black and white textures lurked behind the fog, moving, yet remaining in front of her. A tormenting titter echoed enjoyment of fear's manifestation in the girl.

Not feeling the blade or anything touch her, Abbie shook the fog clear. It dissipated at her vision's center and in the vignette was Mr. Thummel, crouched, cutting the rope from around her legs.

The vignette remained, rendering Abbie to see only in part; the poor girl experiencing this through cataracts vision and an equally cloudy brain. In a fog of war, she was, no doubt. If this wasn't war, then she didn't know what was.

But, she knew. And with her legs now freed, instinct kicked in and she kicked. Glancing blows across Gomez's shins didn't seem to bother him. A wrong adult didn't know this was wrong; she knew it now. Another titter of enjoyment proved it so.

In a blur, he arose—along with him, a silver streak of the knife, coming within a half-inch of her nose. Caught off guard as she was, there wasn't time to react. The proximity of the blade near her eyes obstructed her vision. Delayed, she kicked his legs. The silver near her eyes angled, reflecting light, then moved away from her face as he went around her—

Was he skipping? Abbie thought. *A grown man skipping?*

Yes. Not gracefully. And not through tulips. This dance belonged in a pumpkin patch under a full moon. Wrong was wrong—and this was wrong—backasswards wrong. What was done was done, and it couldn't be undone.

Not able to see him—or the knife—scared Abbie worse than the weirdo waving the steel in front of her. At least she knew—

A tug and the rope tightened around her wrist as he worked on cutting her hands free. Frightened to the point of crapping her bowels and possibly turning her body inside-out, she pulled and yanked, trying to free herself.

Suddenly, the knife glinted in front of her face. So close that the cutting edge of the blade threatened her eyes—and winked at her. Her warring stopped, just as Gomez knew it would.

The blade moved down, scraping her nose as it passed, over her mouth in a cold kiss, and rested, intimidatingly, under her chin. Mr. Thummel raised the cutter, and so did the girl with it, as he knew she would. Once she sat as erect as she could without standing, the knife slid out from under her chin and she felt tugging on the rope near her hands once more.

More scared than at any other time in her life—even

after her father's death—she thought, *They're going to kill me. I need to run!*

Where impatience had gotten the best of her before, an almost accepting calm had her waiting patiently. This moment might be the calmest she had ever been in her life. And she didn't like it. It was *too* calm if there was such a thing. Eerie. And accepting of what? This? Death? Had *flight* warred with *fight* and won? Not flight as in flee, but flight as in actual flight when the spirit departs the dead body and flies to wherever spirits go. A ground-cursed caterpillar got its wings. Did a bell ring? Bye, bye, butterfly.

It might come to that. But acceptance was surrendering. Be damned if that was what Abbie was going to do. As she felt her hands separate in freedom, she launched forward out of the chair, slipped on some leaves, and bolted for the back door.

Holding the knife, Mr. Thummel stood out of a hunch behind the chair and announced, "Ten seconds 'til midnight!"

Standing between Abbie and the door was Mrs. Thummel, who let Mister have his fun. A resolver, she would have liked getting on with it, but it amused her while she waited for midnight. Nothing ever happened before then, anyway.

Here came Abbie, attempting to outmaneuver Missus. Agile herself, Mrs. Thummel stepped between the girl and the door, grabbed her by the shoulders, and looked at her with an expression mixed with excitement, fear, and love—a strange combination that stopped Abbie's fight. It hinted that the woman knew something that Abbie didn't.

Confused, Abbie muttered, *"What?"*

Mr. Thummel came from behind, grabbed Abbie's

arm, and yanked. Abbie's arm firmed against it and when she half-turned around, the knife, in his other hand, was raised above his head.

Time slowed in near suspension, and there they posed: Mrs. Thummel touching one of Abbie's shoulders while standing between Abbie and the back door; Abbie half-turned, leaning back and looking up; and Mr. Thummel holding the knife above his head, postured to swing it down.

All of the uncertainties: of Mister, Missus, and October midnight, outnumbered Abbie.

Then, words, uncertain to the teenager in meaning, but known by the Thummels—for they did know something that Abbie didn't—uttered out of Mrs. Thummel's mouth at that moment, deliberately slow and spaced to avoid any confusion or misinterpretation, "It's—midnight—dear!"

October Midnight

16

October Midnight arrived. Halloween transitioned into All Hollows' Day; the gap, separating the living and the dead, narrowed, allowing the deceased to crossover from the realm of the dead to roam once more among the living on Earth.

A roaring sound upstairs shook the house as if a tornado had blown off the roof and whirled on the second floor.

Abbie looked up at the kitchen ceiling, worried a twister had formed in a nearby field and funneled its way to the only house around to destroy it.

Tornados were about as frightening as anything the world could conjure up. Usually, they made such a racket, it was impossible not to hear them coming and just because it wasn't in view at the time wasn't any indication that it was invisible. Of course, it wasn't. It was there, in its cyclone-hell glory, seeking whom and what it could destroy.

The Thummels, facing up, weren't worried. No, not even an iota and the Missus exuded an anticipatory excitement found on children's faces on Christmas morn.

Whatever was up there unraveled out of its funnel and blew in all directions as if it had exploded, evidenced by an invisible force powerful enough to stress-test the house's structure, which creaked and squealed as if all of the nails were being pulled out of its frame simultaneously.

That would be too meticulous, wouldn't it? Dismantling a home nail-by-nail? Sure it would. Damn impossible for a homewrecker like a twister to do. No, these vortexes of violence snapped wooden frames easier than a black belt in karate, kicking through a wooden skewer the width of a toothpick. Something bloody strange roamed the second floor.

Not anymore. It flew down the stairs faster than a speeding locomotive through a tunnel. Loud, too. Bangs and crashes of glass, no doubt the picture frames, hanging above the steps. A death zone the stairs had become, where frames dismantled and cut through the air like flying daggers, shards of glass as knife blades, rounded sections like throwing stars, and crumbs like shrapnel. Pain occupied there—lots and lots of pain for any flesh-body willing to venture there.

Whatever ripped the place apart was now on the first floor—with the people, who knew exactly where it was because the front door banged inside-out in its frame. All ears in the kitchen had followed its path of destruction; all eyes had followed what they couldn't see. Abbie stared at the door because that's where the last sounds were coming from, not because she saw anything. The Thummels, on the other hand, stared as if they could see the cause.

And what they saw, Abbie didn't want to see. All she knew for sure was that it wasn't a tornado. A twister doesn't descend stairs or bounce off doors. Still, the originator of this havoc, hidden in the wind or possibly invisible itself, was bad news and getting away from it was the best thing to do. So, when Abbie turned around for the back door, Missus stopped her and Mister grabbed her from behind.

Obviously, the Thummels had missed the evacuation memo. Their intention of staying stunned Abbie's understanding of what made sense and what didn't. Leaving made sense; staying computed as illogical. That's what they were—brainless chowderheads, too thick to eat, or else it would clog the esophagus and cause her to choke.

Abbie fought to get away. She was no chowderhead. Hell, the girl hated chowder of any kind. But Mr. Thummel tightened his arms around her as if doing the Heimlich.

"What's wrong with you people!" Abbie yelled. "We have to get out of here."

"Quiet her," Mrs. Thummel said.

Only she didn't look at her husband. Nor at Abbie. Her eyes witnessed something beyond. Something behind. Something approaching.

"Wonderful, aren't they," Mrs. Thummel whispered. *"Oh, oh."*

It wasn't said entirely with fear. Instead, this

sounded more like awe. Utter, genuine *wonder* as Missus had said.

Abbie tried turning around to see it. The impulse felt wrong—so wrong—as wrong as the Earth abandoning its axis and orbit. One minute, she wanted to leave, now, she wanted to see, for seeing was believing.

Mr. Thummel's arms braced her arms against her body like restraining belts on a gurney. One of his wife's fingers poked Abbie's right eye when she reached to hold the girl's head without bothering to look because she was looking elsewhere, behind the girl down the hall.

Moving much quieter now, the presence in the house amounted to nothing more than a gentle breeze. Even though Abbie couldn't see it, she knew it to be true. Mentally following its path came naturally to her, for she had passed through the hall many times, wandering the house. A slight wisp of a flip of an end of a discolored doily curled over as it passed by. A shattering on the floor of a knick-knack falling off an accent table onto the floor. Then a small lamp. A bang sounded, startling Abbie. Not only the sound, but she knew what had caused it. The invisible, moving down the center hall toward the kitchen—toward her, had brushed a hanging picture off the wall. The squeak of a hanging mirror rotating on its nail but holding on.

The mirror was doing better than Abbie. With Mister holding onto her for dear life and Missus restraining her head like a vice, Abbie's free will to hold on or do anything no longer existed, robbed from her. In this world, invisible things were taken at any time and by anybody. All of the unseens: belief, faith, desire, and will existed in people's lives one moment only to be snatched the next.

There was no denying that the Thummels were strong. That played into Abbie's obedience. But, oh, that unsanitary knife, still in Mr. Thummel's hand as he retained her, camouflaged with a pattern of reflective silver and dark gray splotches erect before Abbie's body. No doubt the perve had an erection, but, thankfully, so far, Abbie hadn't felt anything against her backside. A microscopic member, perhaps. Deserving, wouldn't it be, for such a tall, lanky son of a bitch?

A cold breath touched the back of Abbie's neck as if someone had moved the fridge closer and opened the freezer. The taller Mister behind her blocked most of it, but there was no mistaking it was there—or where it came from.

"You better *ru…*" Mister started to say but couldn't finish.

Gusts of wind, more blustery than what Abbie had felt getting out of the car, blew around her on both sides, but nothing directly against her back, for Mister was there. Between him holding her body, missus bracing her head, and the wind applying equal force at her sides as it whizzed by, she remained upright.

The resurging wind repeatedly shoved Mister's right shoulder blade, pushing him into the girl, and pushed Missus' shoulders, creating space between her and Abbie. Both adults struggled to stay on their feet, fighting the wind now as much as trying to hold Abbie.

The gap between the females widened. Missus' hands came off Abbie's head and grabbed her shirt to keep her from being blown back. Multiple forces of pushing, pulling, and racing by caused Abbie's body to sway in an undecided turbulence, bringing on a feeling of motion sickness.

Until this wind forced Mister around Abbie; his arms reluctantly came off the teenager as if being separated from a rock by gushing water carrying him away, turning him around. His momentum took him into his wife, who failed to hold onto the sitter; the knife lost somewhere in the confusion.

Unable to fight the force, the Thummels were driven back toward the backdoor.

It was strange; the wind seemed to ignore Abbie, concentrating its nagging torment on the grown-ups.

What goes around, comes around. In mere seconds, their wills had been snatched by the *will-burglar*, who alone carried out his wishes he had for them. They were at the mercy of … who? … what? …

God? Abbie wondered. *To save me?*

For a moment, the invisible began to materialize, a streaming bluish-gray vapor, dense but without form. What could be seen resembled water flowing through a transparent pipe at a high speed. Still, hard to make out, but it was unmistakably there. Where there had been two flows, now there seemed to be only one, a continuous flow, pushing the adults toward the backdoor.

And then, the vapor crisscrossed within itself, weaving a pattern, as if—what—making a selection? Was it possible?

Sure it was. The force flow distinctly separated into two: one pushing Missus, the other Mister. Abbie saw the whole thing. The impossible made possible by something she didn't understand.

Whether the wind-streams had made their selection or not, they flowed directly into the Thummels. From Abbie's perspective, she couldn't tell whether or not they went through their bodies, exiting somehow. But based on the lack of impact on the door and surrounding wall, it was reasonable to conclude that they didn't pass through.

Which meant what? Abbie couldn't answer. All she knew was what she saw. And what she saw wasn't right. Neither was this. In unison, each stream experienced an explosion inside their flow as if a chemical reaction disagreed. Brilliant light burst and spread out of each, yet, on this weird crossover of day one into day two of Allhallowtide, no sound accompanied the glory. A sonic boom seemed fitting for such outbursts, but the sight without the noise made it all the more eerie for Abbie.

Worse than the lack of sound, the eruptions had increased the flow speed of the streams, racing faster now into both adult's chests as if being sucked into them by a high-powered vacuum, lifting them off their feet and slamming their backs against the kitchen door. A split-second later, the back of their heads cracked against the wood. The knife flew out of Mr. Thummel's relaxed hand and slid across the linoleum floor. Simultaneous with the knife, both of their bodies slid down the door to the floor and stopped, just as soon as the knife stopped under the kitchen table.

With their bodies leaning against the door, legs flat on the floor, arms relaxed, and heads cocked to a side, the last of the bluish-gray vapors finished streaming into them.

Abbie stared, unable to reconcile what the hell had happened. To her, they appeared dead. She wished them dead. There was no sign of breathing.

Interrupting all other thoughts, *I need to run*, flashed red alert in Abbie's mind. In a higher state of awareness, she could feel the tingle of adrenaline spreading through her body. Both stimuli overwhelmed her into paralyzed inaction.

Assuming her previous flee attempt was of the utmost importance. So, fighting against herself, Abbie took a step toward the back door. Why there?—the Thummels were blocking it. Still, any movement was better than none.

Her body agreed and took over, ignoring commands from the mind, turning her around and running in the opposite direction. It felt strange, this disconnect of mind and body. Downright disorienting, the body rebelling against the mind, carrying her away down the same hall she had ventured numerous times throughout the night to the foyer where she hoped it would be the last time. But, essentially kidnapped by her own flesh and blood, who knew if it would be the last time or not.

How she got there didn't matter. What mattered was the front doorknob wouldn't turn. It was locked. Simple enough under normal circumstances, but the answer didn't come easy.

After struggling with what to do, she turned the lever and opened the door. Abruptly, it stopped, pulling something that shouldn't be pulled in her shoulder because of her death grip on the knob. Worse, it triggered heightened panic alarms throughout her already disobeying body on the verge of shock.

Looking out the gap in the door, Abbie saw the remnants of the night after Halloween. Purplish night. Howling wind raking leaves across the ground, occasionally lifting them into the air, twirling, looping. Bare trees gnarled worse than fingers of a witch.

But the cornfields tonight, boys and girls. Nothing but harvested cornfields. Cornfields galore. Vast land between the Thummels' place and another living soul. No one in earshot. It may as well be the Sahara Desert out there.

It took too much time for her to notice the chain still clasped. *Mucho grande* time. All because the boots *panic* and *near shock* stomped on her mind and kicked her ass, about to put her down for the count.

That was the Thummels' plan, wasn't it? To put her down. *'Because, my dear, the story dies with you,'* the Missus had said. There was no risk in explaining her criminal intent to the sitter when the stupid girl wouldn't be around to snitch.

But Abbie wasn't stupid, just experiencing a fear she never knew existed. As she reached up to undo the chain, uncoordinatedly fumbling with it, a wind—from inside the house—blew by her and slammed the door shut.

Abbie screamed bloody murder, *"NOOOOO!"*

Retreating from where it had come, the wind blew passed her again, blowing her hair back and drying her sweat while she yelled.

Nothing left in the *yell-tank*, she leaned forward against the door, exhausted, surprising herself that she didn't collapse right there as she had done hours ago on the landing.

The wind was gone, the house still. The only noticeable noise came from her breathing.

Open the door. Just—open the door.

After her mental voice, amid her breathing, a scraping sound from nearby tightened every muscle in her body. *Outside. It must be something outside. The wind.*

It sounded too faint to come from outside. So, when Abbie looked down at the doorknob and reached for it, the locking-lever was turning on its own.

Staring, she retracted her hand and backed away from the door. A few steps in retreat, something against her back stopped her progress. Twirling around, she screamed.

17

The Thummels stood there, eyeing the young girl.

Knowing her life depended on it, Abbie pleaded, "*Pleeease* let me go!" Her eyes drifted up the stairs. "Think of your kids!"

"*Um. Um.* They don't have to think about us," Mr. Thummel said—only the voice wasn't his own, but that of a young boy.

"*Yeah!* We're, *um*, right here," Mrs. Thummel said in a young girl's voice.

"Where?" Abbie asked, delirious.

"Inside them, dummy," the boy's voice said as Mr. Thummel pointed his thumb back at himself.

"*Yeah*, you're stupid," the girl's voice said out of Mrs. Thummel, whose aged face scowled like a child's.

Abbie screamed, cried, and laughed almost all at once. Her faculties hadn't loosened entirely, but the primary screw holding her together had unscrewed several turns in the last few seconds.

"Mr. and Mrs. Thummel," Abbie barely spoke. "*Pleeease*, stop this. I'm scared, all right. You got me. I'll never fall for one of those sitting ads again."

Mrs. Thummel's adult mouth moved as a young girl's voice spoke out of it too fluid to be lip-synced. "*Um.* Don't call me that. My name is Kaleigh."

"*Yeah.* And my name is Kayne," a high-pitched voice said out of Mr. Thummel as if he had just suffered a blow from steel-toed boots to the *cojones*.

Abbie collapsed to the floor, unable to comprehend what she saw and heard.

Kaleigh crouched down in the adult body quickly and easily with her hamstrings resting on her calves as kids do. "What's your name?"

As Abbie stared at the mismatch of body and voice, Kaleigh's facial features emerged within and through Mrs. Thummel's face, reminding Abbie of the female prop and seeing a video of a terrified woman's face appearing through the skinned-over face, begging, *"Let me out!"*. It brought on that same twitch in Abbie's head and vibration in her heart she had experienced earlier that had floored her prostrate on the landing.

Only Kaleigh's face, hovering within her mother's, wasn't a video. Far from. They both looked equally real. Too real. And too damn blasphemous. No one should see such a thing. Mannerisms and expressions of a child's face underlying an aged adult face with red eyes to boot deformed Mrs. Thummel's appearance, making her human-like at best—but not human. Sub-human, as from below, the deepest recesses of Satan's lair where hell's rejects were exiled for all of eternity.

Something so grotesque and otherly-human should

not be allowed above the surface where humans dwell and it can be seen. This thing had no right to be up here with the living, yet here it was. Somehow it had escaped hell. But this thing didn't want out of the body it occupied no more than criminals committing another crime to return to the big house. *Free spirit*, phooey! This spirit liked the confinement of a body—where spirits belonged.

The little girl's voice coming out of the adult mouth couldn't be believed. Abbie didn't. Seeing wasn't always believing, especially when it's something unnatural, difficult to comprehend, and hard to look at.

Her screw a little looser, Abbie answered, "My name is Abbie."

'Abbie.' The sound of her name acknowledged she was still alive—and awake—for she never succumbed to the twitch and vibration that had caused her to blackout earlier. Hearing her name had even retightened the screw, holding her together, a couple of turns.

Turning away from the two-entity, one-bodied possession, she got up off the floor and ran upstairs, crunching glass, wood, and plastic from the destroyed pictured frames, before her screw loosened again and her sanity, framed by society, fell off the wall, losing her framework to operate within. To her surprise, both doors of the kids' bedrooms were half-way open. *Opened just enough for a six-year-old to go through*, Abbie calculated, then soberly deduced, *They heard the poem.*

Creaking, at the bottom of the stairs, scared her into one of the kids' rooms and she quietly locked the door. When she turned around, darkness tinted the room, but she could still tell it was a boy's room—Kayne's. As displaced as this night had been, it continued with a bookcase out and away from the wall at an awkward angle, cock-eyed and out-of-place. She listened for footsteps coming up the stairs but didn't hear any.

Why rush? They had her, didn't they? For she had confined herself. Even locked herself in. Like a repeat offender, who finds it easier to be handed food, clothes, and shelter, compliments of taxpayers, and maybe a little companionship at the *hôtel de la prison* instead of fending for themselves.

Damn that pesky screw. Now wasn't the time to trust her senses. Who knew if the damned things were accurately sensing things or not. The creak she had heard at the foot of the stairs might have been a creak inside her head. Maybe a creak of a screw turning.

Stepping lightly, she went over to the bookcase. The wall behind it appeared dark, so when she placed a hand on the case to take a closer look, it moved. With one hand, one side of the cabinet swung open farther away from the wall, quietly and smoothly; the knickknacks on the shelves remained put for the ride.

It must be on hinges or something, she reasoned, *well-oiled hinges. Like when dad used to go around the house with a blue and yellow can now and again, spraying things.*

With the case moved out as far it would go, it became clear why the area behind it appeared darker than the rest. It was because there wasn't a wall where the bookcase went. That section had been carved out, possibly for an access point for the large, silver canister, contrasting and filling the dark, recessed space like a colossal bullet lodged in a chamber of a gun instead of a can inside a closet.

As she stepped forward for a closer inspection, her mind and heart contracted in reaction to seeing a distorted image of a form moving toward her out from the inner hollows of the house. Someone or something else was in the room with her.

Instead of getting away from the thing, fear adhered her feet to the floor like a fly to flypaper.

Only after moving her head and arms did she realize the form staring back at her was her reflection in the mirror-like canister.

Holy Ghost, Mary, and Joseph—a love triangle—coming to a church near you! How bizarre could this night get? Very—apparently. As backasswards as Jesus' birth father being a spirit. Still, the Nazarene grew up with two dads, which, depending on the father, may be better than one and without a doubt better than none—as Abbie could attest—because she had a good dad, who kept those hinges lubed and mom's jewelry untangled.

Maybe he liked smelling the stuff—an addict to an elixir that may have caused his death. All Abbie knew was he had died from cancer. What type and where no one had ever said. *Why didn't I ask?*

Inquisitive now, she peeked farther inside the dead-space; her eyes adjusted to the dark. When she touched the canister, it felt like smooth metal. Reflective as it was, it reminded her of a smaller version of a tank on a milk truck. A couple of pipes, connectors, a small box, and a gauge were attached to it on a side.

A sound at the door. Abbie's head snapped in that direction to no avail, only seeing the back of the bookcase, blocking her view.

Stepping back to see the door, Abbie struggled with where to go. What to do was easy. Survive. Life broken down to its simplest element. Her father, Oliver, home, school, and all of their challenges poofed away into oblivion, not carrying any more weight than the air molecules they rode out on. Oh, if only she could have seen their insignificance before now. Not that death was insignificant. It was as significant as anything—and final. But she wasn't dead and that made all of the difference. Her life could still be better, complete, and happy. The choice was her's, no one else's.

Sure, one end of the world had puked on her, the other had shit on her and urinated on her now (keeping in mind that the ends of the circled Earth are many). But it was in her power to laugh after crying and clean herself up rather than letting it dry-crust on her like concrete, forever entombing her in that state. When Oliver rolled around in some poop, they cleaned him up. So, why shouldn't she take equal care of herself?

Resolute to live, Abbie snuck over to the door, stood, and listened. Even though she didn't hear anything in the hall, a voice inside her head whispered that she needed to get out of the room. No revelation there, but at least whatever spoke to her agreed, and that made her feel not so alone. Another thing she wished she had latched onto before this bizzaro night.

No question, the Thummels knew she was up there, so why were they waiting so long to come up—and kill her? What could they possibly gain by dragging this out?

Abbie didn't know. All she knew was it gave her time to think of something. And there it was—regret. Instead of thinking about the past: her father, Oliver, and other stuff, she should have been thinking of a plan. People do that all the time. Little do they know it's robbing time when they give into it. It was something she needed to stop doing herself and stop it right now—before it was too late.

Now, her brain was working. It hadn't occurred to

her prior that maybe the room had another door, a way of escape.

Or, Jesus! A way in. That's why the Thummels were so quiet.

Quickly and quietly, Abbie ventured beyond the bookcase the best she could in the dark toward the back of the room. Within the same wall as the metallic canister was another door, unframed and painted the same color as the wall. The knob the only giveaway that it could open.

Were the Thummels on the other side, waiting for her? Possibly. Hell, anything was possible tonight, including surviving.

When she went to turn the knob, it turned. As the door swung open, it unveiled another room, one with things, big and small, scattered all over the floor. She entered and immediately knew what they were. Toys. Oodles of them. Boys and girls. A playroom.

Bang!

Abbie's head jerked around. The sound came from Kayne's bedroom door. Frantically looking around, snapping her eyesight here-and-there, she found another knob, which meant a door, also unframed and the same color as the room.

Kayne's bedroom doorknob rattled. A Thummel shook it, followed by another *Bang!*, probably Mister, pounding on the door.

Abbie opened the door in the playroom and tiptoed through into the other bedroom—Kaleigh's. It had been a connecting door of a shared playroom situated between the kid's rooms. Her eyes performed a quick scan as she contemplated her next move.

It didn't take long, because her opponents had two checkers left and her only one—herself—trapped in a corner she had no chance of getting out of. They had the spaces covered—the rooms—which meant it wouldn't be long until they converged, ending the game.

Deteriorating fear dissolved much of the time she had left in the game when she saw Kaleigh's bedroom door ajar. Panic swept much of the hope she had gained right out of her. Her mouth was dry from the lack of liquid intake, being open, not talking, and hope's dust. Her vision panned the room only moments at a time before returning to the door. Back-and-forth, they bounced, keeping watch.

No one was in the room with her. The door appeared to be ajar about the same width as when she had come upstairs. Just big enough for a child to squeeze through.

Through the opening, shadows of movement played their tricks. One or both were out in the hall. There was no way she could get to the door in time; it was too far.

Where to go? There's no place to go!

The Thummels were closing in. Closing in to end the game.

18

Abbie searched for a place to hide, a place to prolong life. Under the bed was no good. Neither was the closet, an upright casket. Kaleigh's room also had a bookcase, mirroring the same location in the wall shared with Kayne's room. It's ajar, just not as far as Kayne's was.

As she headed there, the thought, *Ajar enough for a child to go through*, stopped her. After the hesitation, she continued, opened the bookcase farther, stepped inside the hidden dead-space beside the canister, and pulled the case closed, hearing it latch. Slowly, her hand backed away, ready to grab it if it should reopen.

It remained closed. Good thing, because a squeak sounded from Kaleigh's room. Most likely, the door being opened.

Stepping carefully into the darkness of the hidden

space within the walls between the bedrooms, Abbie made her way deeper into the hollow towards Kayne's room. The smooth metal of the canister felt cool to the touch, making her wonder, *What's inside?* She pulled Kayne's bookcase closed, feeling and hearing it catch.

All Abbie could do now was wait and listen. If anything happened to her, it would be her own fault for going upstairs and trapping herself within the house walls.

Creaks sounded from Kaleigh's room, someone walking through, getting warm to Abbie's location in this sick game of hide-and-seek.

Now, banging sounded from the playroom. Then, a faint voice of someone talking to themselves. A girl's, Kaleigh's, carried because of its high pitch. Noises and talking persisted, the woman-girl carrying on as if— playing.

Uncontrollably, Abbie expelled pent-up air along with some fluids, imagining Mrs. Thummel moving about the room—playing—with toys like a six-year-old.

Bang!

Abbie jumped.

It sounded like it came from Kayne's bedroom door. Each pound on the door echoed in Abbie's heart, jolting her body. The boy was unaware of his strength, using the body of a grown man, his father's. It must be like a regular guy all of a sudden having superpowers.

Abbie pulled out her cell phone and used it as a flashlight. It wasn't necessary to ask why she hadn't thought of it before. Who could think straight under these circumstances? She used it now, that was all that mattered.

After seeing what was around her, she pointed the light above her head. There appeared to be some type of hatch. *An attic?* crossed her mind, but she knew she couldn't stay up there forever. *Up there* might be worse than *in here*. Breaking through a window and having to jump off the roof might be asking too much, even if her life depended on it.

Angling the light to the floor, she was surprised to see there wasn't one. Luckily, her feet stood on wooden beams spaced around the center of the canister to support it. She was standing beside only the top half of the metal tank with the whole bottom half below her feet. There was no mistaking it. The gaps between the beams allowed plenty of light to reach down and reflect off the metal. How she missed them, she didn't know.

The height and view messed with her balance, so she coveted the canister. In doing so, the cell phone fell out of her hand, through a gap, pinged against the metal can, and landed somewhere down below. Her breathing and body stilled as she closed her eyes in regret. Any hope the panic broom had failed to sweep out of her earlier fell through that gap with her phone. *They heard that! They know where I am!*

Hurried, heavy steps made their way from the hall into Kaleigh's bedroom. *Kayne. Kayne heard.* They stopped near his sister's bookcase.

If the case opened, Abbie didn't think she would be able to contain her fear. Tears and sweat soaked her face; a face turned red from holding in everything she wanted to spew out.

Mere seconds had fooled her into thinking long spans of time had passed. Apparently, Kayne had failed to notice the closed bookcase and didn't bother to open it. If the Thummels didn't kill her, the suspense would.

It sounded like Kaleigh was still playing in the

playroom until heavy pounding across the floor drowned it out. Kayne had gone to the playroom.

This is my chance! Abbie thought. Her luck in this unlucky situation renewed some hope that she might make it. Until she heard from the playroom—

"Kaleigh, *um*, *wh*—*why* didn't you come get me?"

Abbie didn't have to be there to see it. For she had seen it downstairs, stabbing the brain through the eyes too close and up the keister too damned personal. The boy's voice speaking out of a grown man kept her in the hollow of the house a bit longer.

Then, she heard, "I was playing," Kaleigh answered.

Mrs. Thummel, the real one, the one who had returned with Mister, wasn't the playing type. Backward as ass-backward because if they ever moved forward like a car, they did so in reverse.

"Yeah, but you still could have *gu...gu...gotten* me," Abbie heard Kayne say.

"But I was playing," Kaleigh explained.

"*Oh, okay.* Can I play with you?"

Abbie went to open the latch to Kaleigh's bookcase, thinking the door would still be open, when she overheard Kaleigh say, "I want to play with Abbie."

Everything Abbie had wanted to release earlier, all of the pressure and gunk congested in her head, nearly exploded then. If it had, it surely would have turned her inside out.

"I want to play," Kayne begged as if he would be excluded.

"Okay. You can play, too."

"*Wha...what* do you want to play?"

"Hide and seek."

"Hide and seek?"

"Yeah. You were it, and you found me, now we

need to find Abbie."

"*Oh*, okay."

Abbie heard the sound of toys falling to the floor, then heavy steps from Kaleigh and Kayne running through Kaleigh's bedroom.

Abbie knew she had missed an opportunity to leave. She also knew now why the Thummels hadn't come upstairs right away earlier: they were busy playing hide and seek with each other. Now, they were looking for Abbie. But, it was as if they weren't themselves. Perhaps, they had forgotten about the kitchen and their plans to kill her. Maybe, an invisible horseshoe hung around the sitter's neck. And maybe, someone had placed a rabbit's foot in her pocket without her knowing. Maybe, she'd find a penny on her way out of the house and pick up an acorn outside for good measure.

And *maybe*, the Thummels will pick up that knife from under the kitchen table and take turns stabbing each other until they both died. What a worthless word: *maybe*—and all of its synonyms. Such words conjured up hope, but the *false* kind. Trade it in for *certainty*; the less *uncertainty,* the better.

Nice try. Life equaled uncertainty. And most of the time, risks outweighed the reward—what a shitty environment. So, there comes a time when getting out of that environment was the only thing to do—before someone flushed the toilet. It's important.

Hell, even a girl in high school knew that. Not all kids were dumbasses. Abbie had known all along that getting out of the house was the best way to try to survive. So far, it's been a bitch trying to make it happen. Oh, she had touched many a door handle, namely the back and front, but that's as far as she had gotten. Even had the front door opened once. But when doors locked themselves, who could compete with that?

Abbie, that's who—if she wanted to live. Already at the risk of dying, taking the chance to be rewarded with more life wasn't a risk at all. So, here we go.

19

Honestly, when the cell phone fell, the last thing Abbie thought was whether it still worked or not. But it did. Its light shined up toward her like an illumination marking the spot. *Maybe*, instead of walking out of one of the bedroom doors and out the front or back door like everything was normal, *maybe*, heading down toward the phone might lead to another way out. *Maybe...Maybe...Maybe...*

The beams around the canister looked solid and Abbie guessed she could fit through some of those gaps. Squeezing between the metal canister and the wooden beams, she lowered her body through. Her own body blocked the light shining up, making it difficult to see and judge. Nothing she could do about it, she carried on, holding onto a wooden beam into a straight-armed hang, her body dangling.

Nothing left to grab and the phone's light closer than it had been, she let go.

Her sneakers smacked the surfaced when she landed, only falling a foot or so. It had seemed farther—it always does. Picking up the phone and shining it above her, she had estimated right: the shiny can was about double her height.

The surface under her handled her fall, but how sturdy it was was anyone's guess. So, mentally, she tried to make herself lightweight to take some of the load off. The powerful suggestion of the mind. Oh, if that really worked.

With just enough room to crouch down, she saw a crawlspace. It looked big enough for her to fit through, probably an adult male could, too, some kind of access way, which gave her confidence in the sturdiness of the wood under her. Shining the phone light down it, she hoped the only thing crawling in that crawlspace would be her.

Either way, there wasn't a choice was there? From what she could tell, the only other way out of there was up from where she came. That wouldn't work, so, on all fours, she crawled into the wooden shaft, making sure her hands and knees used the two-by-fours for additional support.

When Abbie came to the end of the crawlspace, nothing had bothered her along the way, not even a spider web or cobweb. It was if the shaft had been what? ... *cleaned* not long ago. How else could she explain the lack of dust on the lumber and boards? She couldn't, but she was thankful. Like most teenage girls, arachnids, bugs, and insects made her skin crawl and that always made her feel like they were on her, although they weren't.

Her dropped phone had taken her down; a folded attic ladder at the end of the shaft suggested the same thing. When she pushed down on it, the ladder and a board underneath moved down, spring-loaded, but where did it lead?

Abbie waited, unsure if the Thummels had heard it move. They must not have, so there was only one way to find out where this went, and that was to take a peek.

On her hands and knees with her butt in the air, she pushed down on the ladder and lowered her head between the rungs for a look. At this angle, there was nothing helpful to see. The door under the ladder blocked a lot from view. Pushing the ladder and door down until she could see was her only option.

Doing so, this could get nastier than popping a zit, but what needed to be done, must be done. What choice did she have?

Pushing down on the ladder-door again until she saw something resulted in opening it nearly the entire way. Anyone down there would see it. No getting around it—no taking it back. What needed to be done was done and couldn't be undone. That was the worst sometimes.

In this case, it worked out. Not a Thummel in sight, not a Thummel in sound. Not a Thummel around, to see the ladder go down.

Unless they were being stealthy little bastards in big bastard bodies.

Doubtful, but it was plenty dark with low visibility. Until Abbie used the light of her phone. There was some kind of landing below and possibly a door to the left. Definitely not any of the main living quarters of the house. This was someplace new, someplace she hadn't been.

A stench, similar to the one she had noticed in the kitchen after arriving that had reminded her of old people, ascended into the crawlspace and invaded her nostrils. A stagnant staleness of death must be throughout the house. Though, only where people dwell—the living areas—because prior to opening the hatch, the hollow of the house hadn't smelled like that.

With the ladder-hatch down and no one coming to tag her, Abbie turned herself around in the crawlspace and proceeded down the ladder onto the landing. Her eyes hadn't deceived her. The light of her cell phone shined on three walls, a door built in the left, and steps. Beyond the light's reach, it was reasonable to think there were more steps, but beyond them, who knew what hid in the darkness? Only a musty, old basement she hoped.

Abbie checked the battery life of her phone. Not bad. With no service, no calls going in or out, no emails or other notifications, it was lasting pretty well. Besides, she just charged it before leaving the house.

But that was hours ago. Her body battery wasn't doing as well. In fact, it could use a little charging. Some fresh air, drink, food, and sleep would do the trick, but she would settle for the fresh air. It would mean she made it outside. And outside gave her a chance.

Putting an ear against the door, she listened. Nothing, her hand reached down and turned the doorknob. *Please be unlocked. Please be unlocked. Please be unlocked.*

It was, so she turned it, slowly and quietly, all the way and cracked the door for a peek. It was as if she had opened up to a whole new world, one with light, furniture, and—noise—from the Thummels running down the stairs almost directly above her.

Panicked, Abbie closed the door. Not softly, either. Rushed in wanting it closed to have something between her and those *it*, that was all. Usually, being found in hide-and-seek meant you now closed your eyes, counted to a certain number, and looked for hiders so someone new could be *it*. The unfortunate soul found in *this* game of hide-and-seek meant game over for the hider because the kids were always *it*.

Kids. Who was she *kidding?* Herself, that's who, hearing grown bodies stress-test the stairs, take the corner at the foyer like two cross-country racers jockeying for position, and sprinting down the hallway by the basement door, laughing and giggling, for the checkered flag.

A sudden downpour of torrential rain rumbled on the roof. A howling wind, October's wind, pressed against the house, with an underlying whisper sounding all too similar to *Did you miss me?*

No, Abbie did not. The rain and wind made it harder to hear.

Her dropped cell phone had her follow down. So had the lowered ladder. Now, the stairs, descending into darkness, had her venturing down again, below ground. Carefully and quietly, she descended, holding the handrail with her right hand, and the cell phone in her left, using it as a flashlight.

In stopping to scan the light around, the stone wall to her left showed the true age of the house. And, as she approached the bottom of the steps, a dirt floor and washer and dryer in the corner confirmed this was a basement. As if the dirt spoke out of the floor to the dust in her being, a strong, undeniable truth revealed itself that there was no more *down* for the living, only for the dead, who could go another six feet, stop, and rest.

There was no way Abbie would have thought that on her own. Not like that. Not in a zillion years. It was as if the earthy floor had brought in the elements: the rain chilled her bones dead cold and, October's wind dried them, shattered them, and blew her dust into oblivion.

Holy Mother of God, tell your Son to get me out of this mess!

Strange, this experience went deeper than a feeling. Even deeper than imagination. Not only did she see herself shatter into a billion pieces and blow away, she felt it. Standing on dirt at the bottom of the steps of the basement, she unraveled.

Everything that had happened raised their ugly heads all at once and yelled, "Surprise!"

Yes, it was. And not a pleasant one. No, where's a machete when you needed one? These uglies should have their heads chopped off, ground into a soft meal, fed to pigs, shit out, taken to a lab, fed to a waste-eating bacterium, then incinerate the munchers.

Even after all of that, Abbie wasn't sure tonight and these feelings would be gone. Every single ugly that had reared its head seemed superior in every way. Toying with her until they were done playing.

Afraid, Abbie turned and swung the light to her right. Not sure what she had expected, it was safe to say she didn't expect to see what she saw. Metal barrels. A bunch of them. All labeled Gelida Somno Gas.

As she came to the end of the barrels, two large cardboard boxes, the ones the washer and dryer had come in, ended the parade like Santa in his sleigh. When she shined the light into the first, it was filled with many smaller boxes—medical stuff she didn't understand. The other box contained hoses, nozzles, and other rubber and plastic parts. Behind the boxes, a tarped contraption.

As she turned with the light, the rest of the basement was mostly empty, except for a few candles spread out on the floor and a metal folding chair with something draped over the backrest. On her way to the chair, grooves in the dirt floor, like water ruts, were everywhere. At the chair, what resembled a black robe, maybe two, draped over the backrest and a black cup and a box of matches were on the seat.

From this angle, a pattern emerged in the ruts. At first, a circle, the curves easier to see, then straight lines through the circle. Where they crossed, Abbie could make out triangles; black candles on the six outermost points and one at the center of the circle. Letters, squiggly lines, and symbols carved in the dirt meant someone had spent some time creating this.

This what? A hexagram? Pentagram? She couldn't remember which.

The other *witch* was right—as in *witchcraft*. Were the Thummels witches? They looked like they could be. Especially, the Missus. It would explain a lot.

Not really. The knowledge gained from this find only made it worse. Foolish to think stumbling onto something associated with satanic rituals and the like would make it better or even more understandable.

The cultic basement confused Abbie, but it frightened her more.

20

Station Knoll's small population never warranted having a police department, so all calls went directly to the state police with the nearest department in Station Flat, eighteen miles away.

A state police officer, leaning against the counter in the Syfert's kitchen, spoke on the phone with someone at the station, giving them the address of 513 Spooky Nook Road, Station Knoll.

Another officer, taking notes, sat at the kitchen table with Abbie's mom.

"That's a good description of the woman, ma'am," he said. "You never know what may help us find your daughter."

He wrote something then looked up from his notes at Daphne. "Ma'am, can you describe the car this woman was driving?"

"Yes," Daphne answered. "I think so. It was black. Older. I don't know—maybe seventies or eighties. Big ... and long. As kids, we used to them *boats* because they were so big. It was starting to get dark, but it looked like maybe the roof was cloth or vinyl," she said, unsure. "It didn't shine like the rest of the car."

The officer nodded as he wrote.

"Oh. And it had in-state plates."

"Do you remember any of it?"

After frustrated recall failure, she answered, "No. Not all of it. I think it started with *B*? Maybe, a six in there?"

She was guessing, he knew. Still, he wrote them down. A few additional scribbles, logging her uncertainty, the officer looked up from his notes. "Ma'am, do you know the make or model of the car?"

Frustration contorted her face as bulbous tears dribbled down her cheeks. "I'm sorry; I don't." How she wished she knew. How she wished she had one of those photographic memories that captured every detail in a split second. Selfishly for herself *and* her daughter—her baby.

Composed and pointed, the officer continued on the same point from a different angle. "Ma'am. You gave us distinguishable features of the woman. Besides the vinyl roof, was there anything unique about the *car* that caught your attention?"

He was losing her. He had only seen it one other time, but he knew. Her mind raced, searching something, anything, but produced nothing. Because as her mind worked, it also aimed self-producing blame at her, yelling at her from the inside why she couldn't remember, why she hadn't driven Abbie herself, why she had let her go and with a stranger no less, why she had cut out the ad in the first place.

"Scratches," the officer offered, trying to reel her back in. "Dents. A missing hubcap. Cracked window."

Abbie's mother shook her head. Not for a single reason, but for many. For starters, why couldn't she remember? Along with disbelief that she couldn't remember. A feeling of uselessness when her baby needed her. Shock that this was happening after losing her husband and dog so close together. They never made it out of that fog, either, wandering in the past trying to keep better days alive. And rattled. Yes, that's what she heard inside her shaking head—rattling. From more than one screw loose. Brokenness. That's why her brain didn't work. Worry. Fear of being alone. All of that debilitating stuff wasn't helping.

The officer let her be, giving her time without applying any more pressure. For he knew, she had applied too much already on herself. Its weight had sunk her low, stuck in the miry clay.

And judgment, plenty of it, throwing a book of wrongs at herself so big she could open the cover and curl up in it—like a coffin.

Her eyes closed. More of an escape than anything else. As if not seeing the cops in the kitchen would fool her into thinking this wasn't happening. Dumb, really, or really dumb, either way, because she knew well enough she couldn't escape herself. That—

Wait a minute. Wait a minute. Jesus! She's standing on the porch, watching Abbie and Nora get into the car.

"The woman," Daphne said with her eyes closed, "Nora, had to turn the car around."

Adjusting in his seat, the cop jotted it down, hoping more would come and they would be in business.

The other officer on the phone situated a recent

photo of Abbie on the counter.

"Hold on a sec," he said. "Let me take this picture so I can send it over to you."

He snapped a couple of pictures with his phone, reviewed them, then punched a few buttons.

"Alright. Still there? Yeah. Just sent 'em. They're on their way. Yep. Let me know when you get 'em."

Abbie's mom, envisioning herself at the moment on the porch, regretted it right away. She heard Abbie, her baby, say, 'I love you, too, Mom.' Now, that's all she hears. *I love you, too, Mom.' 'I love you, too, Mom.' 'I love you, too, Mom.'*

Please, God! Why are you so cruel? 'I love you, too, Mom.' She's all I have! Don't make me live with this! 'I love you, too, Mom.' She's all I have! I can't! I won't! I'll...

She never saw Abbie waving back or blowing her a kiss from the car because it was too dark. Too dark. *It was getting dark.* It would have been too much remembering such a thing. *Too dark. Dark. Night. Dark night. Black. Death. Curl up in the book of wrongs and close the cover like pulling up a blanket. Black death. Black car. Black death car.*

Daphne opened her eyes. Immediately, they teared up again as if exposed to tear gas and she said, "I think the entire car was black."

In shame, her hands covered her face.

That may have been the last time I ever see my daughter. Last. Time. Last time. Curl up inside the book of wrongs to be read to me as a perpetual reminder...

The officer twiddled the pen in his fingers, then set the pen down on the pad, wondering if he had pushed too hard without knowing he had. Sympathetically he said, "Ma'am. You told us earlier the car was black."

Her face emerged out of her hands as if playing

peek-a-boo.

"No," she said firmly. "I mean, the car was black. *All of it.* The bumpers, the hubcaps, the mirrors— everything looked black."

The officer picked up the pen, started to write, stopped, and said, "Ma'am, it was getting dark, right?"

"Not dark enough to not know the difference between a chrome bumper and a black one."

While writing, he asked, "Like how some Mennonites do with their cars, painting everything black?"

I cut out the ad.

"Yeah, like that."

I handed it to her.

"Everything black."

'You know—get your mind off things.'

21

The basement door opened. Standing in the middle of the hexagram, Abbie frantically looked around for another way out. *No place to hide! Can't go down! Down is for the dead!*

A beam of light shined down the stairs.

I need to run!

The theme of the night, but to where?

Debilitating fear jumbled her thinking. *Dig!* The dirt beneath her feet said. *Dig—your own grave!*

The wooden steps creaked under the weight of the Thummels' adult bodies.

Over there. Blackness. An opening? A void? Like the hollow behind the kids' bookcases?

Running to it, Abbie scuffed part of the hexagram and kicked over a candle. In approaching the void, movement in front of her made her recoil. It was her reflection in the glass of a French-paned door tucked within a recessed doorway.

Peeking through and turning the knob, she confirmed no one was on the other side. The door led outside, but it was locked. Worse yet, padlocked besides.

When she looked out the glass again, it was dark, but she could still make out a landing and concrete steps just on the other side of the door. Steps wet with rain that led to outside—and, *oh, those cornfields!*

Low moans sounded from the steps as the Thummels took their time descending, unsure of Abbie's whereabouts.

Abbie, however, knew right where the Thummels were. And when she had looked over her shoulder toward the stairs, a beam of light, preceding the Thummels, shortened and narrowed on the steps and wall, gauging their progress.

Oh, shit! Oh, God!

Fear had brought a friend because something took Abbie over, possessed her. Counterintuitively, the girl ran back into the basement toward the steps, skidded her sneakers on the dirt when she got to the folding chair, and picked it up, letting the robes, cup, and matches fall to the floor.

The flashlight's beam bounced up and down near the bottom of the steps.

"We found you! We found you!" Kaleigh's excited voice carried through the near-empty basement, as did the pounding of the Thummels' feet, moving them quickly down the stairs.

Oh, God!

The old metal chair collapsed in Abbie's grasp, folded itself from wear and tear, as she ran it back toward the door. In all one motion, she heaved it underhanded with all of her might. Spinning end-over-end like a giant boomerang, the chair broke through the glass and wooden bars of the French-paned door and landed on the bottom base, tilted, like a seesaw at rest: one end on the concrete landing outside, the other in the air inside the basement. Remaining fragmented panes of glass slid out of the door and fell on the chair, spraying glass crumbs on both sides of the door's base.

Then, her shadow cast on the recessed doorway; glass twinkled on both sides of her form like misplaced stars. Her back felt warm, as if the sun shined on it.

Behind her, Mister pointed the flashlight.

Which might as well have been a gun. Instinctive conditioning made Abbie raise her arms; the arms of her silhouette on the wall followed. Not born from personal experience, this reaction seemed to be the right thing to do when caught. It wasn't as if she had done anything wrong, nor was it customary to raise one's arms when found in the game of hide-and-seek. Yet, guilt swept over her just the same. Not from throwing the chair through the door—no, to hell with those witches and their rituals. It came from—

"*Wah…Wah*…We found *yooo*!" Kayne said, excited, out of his father.

Something made Abbie turn around. Blinded by the light, she's not sure how close Kayne and Kaleigh were, but close enough; the sun in her sights grew. Then, seeing red eyes behind the outermost ray of light, she knew everything. Sometimes, everything can be summed up into one thing. And her life boiled down to this: *RUN!*

Abbie turned and ran toward the broken door. Kayne just missed grabbing her before she took off.

It wasn't graceful, but at full speed, Abbie jumped up and out, making herself small, knees and elbows first, her face tucked in the crevice of her arm, through the near glassless door; what glass remained sliced through her clothes and skin.

"Get her, Kayne!" Kaleigh barked.

When Abbie cleared the chair through the bottom of the door, her shins and ankles bore the brunt of an awkward landing on the wet concrete steps outside, along with a tingling and numb elbow, which had broken her fall.

Things hurt—bad. Make no mistake about it; every pain had registered, shouting *here* when her brain had called their name in the roll call, but not fully because her mind concentrated more on getting out of there. And to do that, she needed her body. She would gladly take all of the pain it had to dish out later if she got out of this alive. Injuries didn't matter. Mind over matter. Living mattered. Not only for her but for her mom. So, scrambling on all fours on the slimy steps, she climbed.

For the first time in a long time, Abbie had gone *up* instead of *down*. Up to the backyard and, not far off, those harvested cornfields on all sides—cornfields galore—between her and another living soul, who might help, or at least call the police.

So far, *up* wasn't any better than *down*. A cold, hard rain had soaked her heavy, while October's wind tried knocking her down. Both elements tag-teamed against her, helpers of the Thummels.

But, a start was a start. Abbie had made it out of the house and was running: two things she had tried to accomplish all night.

Everything near the house had a sheen to it from being wet and, up ahead, the grass looked like tinsel under the moonlight. Exactly what direction to head, she wasn't sure. Other than through a cornfield. So few lights. So few houses. Oh, how small they looked in the distance, dwarfed by the fields. No way around the cornfields, only through. It was a long way to go and even longer to run.

"We see you! We see you, Abbie!" one of the kids yelled from behind her, sounding like Kayne.

His voice and doubt that she could outrun him had her veering off into the barn.

Kayne's voice had carried out of the dungeon basement's doorway and up the recessed steps as if spoken through a megaphone. This had led her to believe Kayne was much closer than he actually was.

Still inside the basement, Kayne used the flashlight to break away any remaining glass in the door before he and his sister went through after her. Neither had seen her; neither knew where she was.

Soaked, Abbie splatted water on the barn's concrete floor when she entered, sounding a lot like it does when getting out of the pool. It didn't take long for the dripping to slow, but the damage had been done. For, a water trail had been left for the Thummels to follow.

There was no way the trail was going to dry anytime soon. Not the way it's been raining on and off tonight. She wanted to hide, but she couldn't leave a trail right to her, nor could she stand there. Both ends of the barn were wet from the doors being open. It was the dry area in the middle where there would be a problem.

Yes, a wet sneaker, tread-leaving problem. The rain may as well have been liquor on an underage drinker. It was obvious. Upon entering the barn, the Thummels would know she had been there. At least passing through or if she stayed, they would track the prints to her location.

Oh, that wasn't all. With both ends of the barn open, the moonlight crept in, shedding light fairly deep inside, except for the center.

Abbie knew she was making this easy for her searchers. No doubt, she had been a handful, but enough already. With the rain, October's wind, cornfields galore, the barn, and now her helping them, how could they not get their hands on her?

Maybe not everything was against her. Like why wasn't Kayne at the barn already when he had sounded so close?

To hell with the rain-trail, she had to hide. If the center of the barn was the only option, then she had to make it work. But, entering the darkness beyond moonlight's reach, what did she find? Nothing. Nada. Nil. Not a damned thing. Not even a loft. It made sense now why both end doors were open.

What didn't make sense was where in the hell was Abbie going to hide? It's a little hard to do when there's nothing to duck behind, crawl into, climb up, or anything around to cast a shadow. The only thing doing that was the barn itself.

Another thing was the center of the barn was dark, but not that dark.

Foolishly, her fear of Mister and thinking he was on her tail was what had led her into the barn—a barn where the barn itself was the only hiding place.

I'm tired. So tired.

22

Abbie would have checked the time on her cell phone but didn't want to chance the light giving away her location. Checking both ends of the barn, she couldn't understand where the Thummels were. Maybe she should have kept going. Maybe they hadn't seen her enter the barn.

Maybe...Maybe...Maybe...

Eyeing one end of the barn, then the other, she backed up, knowing there was nothing in the way to trip her except her own two feet. Which was a serious possibility. That shin-knee-elbow-landing on the concrete steps had screamed at first, then moaned, but moaned a little louder now from being still for so long. Tightness in those contused areas choked more pain out of them. If they ever started screaming again, she would be in serious trouble.

Like she wasn't already. Her back hit the wall. In this desolate place, that's all it could have been. Unlike backing into the Thummels in the foyer, where the kids, she was supposed to watch and couldn't find, had decided to make first contact. How? Through their parents, that's how?

How, indeed. But what a first impression.

While Abbie stood with her back against a wall, trying to figure everything out, thunder boomed overhead. Instead of her eyes snapping up toward the sound, they set on one barn door, then the other. Not seeing anyone, they raised toward the barn ceiling. At that moment, rain pummeled the roof in an all-out attack with such force she thought the world had turned upside while the barn stood still and an ocean fell on it.

All she could hear was the rain. Near perfect acoustics inside the barn made it sound louder than it was, but make no mistake, it was raining pumpkins and apples. There was no way she would ever hear the Thummels coming. Not now. Even October's wind had stealthily channeled through, creating a wind tunnel powerful enough to blow the roof off. Or keep it up under the rain's assault. And dry her off if she stood there long enough, maybe those water spots, too.

Then, it occurred to her that if she couldn't hear the Thummels, then they couldn't hear her either. Heavy breathing. Movement.

But they would *see* her in this barren barn. And seeing was believing no matter what was heard.

That killed the momentum she had. Regret filled the void.

Why did I take this job? Why did I come in here? I should have kept running. For the train station. Yes, the train station.

It occurred to her now. *Surely, someone would be there who could help. There'd be no need to go into town.*

It sounded so easy, until picturing herself doing it. *Can I run that far?* No matter how it sounded, imagining it brought on more doubt than belief.

Without being caught? A kid's energy inside an adult body? I'm not sure I can compete with that.

The composition of the Thummels confused and fascinated Abbie. Exactly what that composition composed of wasn't clear, but she figured it entailed an adult body, mind, and spirit, along with a child's— *what?*—spirit and maybe mind—not mind— consciousness? It seemed crowded in there.

Such musing made her question her own composition and whether it was in two parts or three— blessed trinity—they all agreed: *I don't want to—*

Outside the barn door to her right, a beam of light bounced along the ground. The same flight response adrenalized her. *I need to run!*

After a fleeting glimpse of regret from realizing she had stayed in the barn too long, all thinking stopped and Abbie took off running for the opposite door. Savage, she had become. If anyone stepped in front of her, Mister or Missus, she was bowling them over. Maybe not doable with Mister in her frail frame, but it's how she felt. Not invincible, *per se*, more a desire to live. And that, by God, if there was a God, made her dangerous in her own way.

With October's wind at her back, she emerged out of the barn and into the pouring rain, passing Kaleigh, who was about to reach the barn door and enter. Seeing her and those red eyes—*Missus with your eyes so bright, won't you guide the hunt tonight*—made Abbie kick it into another gear. Being able to do that as tired as she was and her body moaning gave her confidence she might make it to the train station.

Barefoot, Kaleigh ran after the sitter, but couldn't keep up. The long black dress, wet and clinging to her body, especially the fabric around her legs, didn't help. Nor did the cuts on the bottom of her feet when she had exited the basement.

With Kaleigh on *this* side of the barn, that meant the beam of light on the other side belonged to Kayne, who, in his pinstriped suit, hightailed it through the barn after Abbie once he saw her. The girl had gotten a good head start on him, but he was off to a good start himself.

With October's wind at his back, he appeared out of the barn and into the rain, resembling a long-stride distance runner, holding the flashlight like a lighted baton.

Accurate, in part, if he were in athletic apparel and sneakers. There was no way of getting around that he also looked like Gomez, wandering the cemetery on a frightful night he would find gorgeous, taking in the family grave markers in all of their various forms, while holding a gigantic cigar, most likely the very thing that would escort him to his own grave.

Abbie had sloshed across the backyard, now in the cornfield, heading in the direction of the train station. A prickling sensation filled her legs.

About to leave the yard and enter the cornfield, Kayne inside Mister made up ground.

The running rhythm with which Abbie had started with began to wane, mostly, in her lower body. Herky-jerky movements, hips swinging side-to-side, knees coming up too high, and unsteady ankles slowed her down. Blame it on a number of things: exhaustion, dehydration, that crash-landing on the steps, the rain, the circumstance, the ruts and chopped off stalks in the cornfield. Those cobb-producing things! Nothing but fields—as far as the eye could see. And her eyesight was fine.

Gaining on her, Kayne felt spazzing in his own legs—Mr. Thummel's legs—his father's. Not a surprise there. Mister had the height and stride to be a good runner, and was once—in high school—but he had already run farther tonight than he had all years prior. And the Missus, *well*, she never ran—*ever*—not on her own since elementary school and only when required in gym class. So, it was up to Kayne inside Mister to get the girl—before his legs cramped.

Closing the distance, Kayne reached for her with his free hand but missed. Needing another gear, Abbie couldn't get her legs to respond. Then, she felt him brush her back. A burst forward put her out of reach again.

They ran like that for some time, no more than a foot or two separating them, through the rain, across a muddy, harvested cornfield. Spectators would be *oohing* and *aahing*, knowing the race would come down to a photo finish.

But there weren't any spectators. No one close by. No one in earshot. The train station still a ways away.

Kayne's foot stepped down and rose without a dress shoe—for it had stuck in the mud and stayed there.

Losing a step or two, Kayne raised the flashlight and threw it at the sitter. Through wind and rain, it tumbled end-over-end, shining its beam on Abbie, the wet ground, back onto himself, and then up into the night sky, illuminating raindrops, as it completed an evolution. The cycle repeated until the light banged into the back of Abbie's head.

Add a flashlight to the back of the head to what amounted to one hell of an injury list. And hell it was because the blow caused Abbie to stumble. A hellish nightmare that wouldn't end until she ended because *'the story ended with her,'* Missus had said.

The Thummels hadn't forgotten and somehow Kayne and Kaleigh also knew. There have been some close families since the dawn of man, but this took the last piece of pumpkin pie off the dessert tray—a family of four in two bodies.

As Abbie stumbled to keep her footing, Kayne caught up and tackled her from behind. The force snapped Abbie's head forward. They fell together and landed together; Abbie first, her face in the mud, clogging her nose, with Mister on her back. As he pushed on her to get himself up, she could feel her body sink into the mud. His bony knees gouged into her lower back. A large hand grabbed the back of her head and pushed her face deeper into the earthy paste.

Dying from suffocation had not crossed Abbie's mind. Stabbed to death by Mister with that goddamn knife in the kitchen had seemed the most likely, but what did she know about death?

Plenty, from her father and Ollie, but this was different for one cosmic differentiating reason: they had died from disease and she was about to die from Mister's hand.

Sure, one could call Mr. and Mrs. Thummel a disease and not be wrong, for they were adversely affecting her as a disease would. A fast-acting illness, snuffing her out of this world.

Another hand pressed against the middle of her shoulder blades, pressing her breasts against the field. A knee gnarled into her lower back; the other surely straight from Kayne bracing himself to exert the most force.

Utilizing the full weight of a grown man, Kayne rammed that knee of his father's into her lower back, forcing any remaining air out of the sitter, jarring her entire body and sinking it deeper into the accepting earth. Earth seemed to know a death was imminent, willing to accept the dust that had been lent to Abbie to roam the Earth for a time.

That was all she was to the boy and his father: *the sitter.* A dumb girl needed for an exchange to fulfill an agreement made long ago.

This is it, Abbie thought. *The story dies with me.*

As she laid face-down in mud up to her ears, struggling to live, a hand grabbed a handful of her wet hair and yanked. Greedily, the mud fought to hold on as if wanting Abbie's dust back. But Kayne's will made Mister too strong. A suction sounded when her face separated from the warring mud. That was the last resistance. Her head swung back easily from the pull. So did her mouth, opening and gasping for air. A heavy rain smeared mud into her eyes.

Abbie may not have died then, but some life had been taken from her. Sure, she fought to breathe, but the last resistance had not been entirely hers. No, there were three fighting for the sitter: Abbie, the earth, and Mister—four if you count Kayne mastering Mister.

With some air in her lungs, eyes closed, Abbie demanded, "LET…" *Huh!* "ME…" *Huh!* "GO!" *Huuuh!*

Saying it had cost her. It expelled breaths that would not be easily replaced. Not with her chest compressed between the ground and the weight of Mr. Thummel.

Carrying Mr. Thummel's dress shoe that had gotten stuck in the mud and the flashlight, Kaleigh inside Missus caught up, shined the light on Abbie, then on Kayne.

"*Aaaaawe!* You're in trouble," she said. "Look at your suit."

"*Ma…ma…mom* doesn't care," Kayne replied. "*I…I…*got her, didn't I?"

Out of Mrs. Thummel's mouth emerged her adult voice when she said, "Mom certainly does care, Mister!"

What had happened to Kaleigh's voice, Abbie didn't know. Hearing it made her wish she hadn't, yet she was alive to listen to it.

There's four of them here, Abbie thought. *I can't take on four.*

The reality was she couldn't take on one—Mister—if it ever came to that. Especially a Mister filled to the gills with Kayne, a boy hell-shelled on ending the game of hide-and-seek and equally hard-cocked on ending her.

Most of the mud felt like it had washed from Abbie's face, so she chanced opening an eye, just in time to see Missus' body bend over, stiff like an adult, not limber like a child as before, so it was Missus at the mind's wheel and not Kaleigh. Those red eyes peeked through gnarled hair like a wolf patiently waiting in a forest, eyeing its prey.

A hand reached toward Abbie. The sitter's lone opened eye widened despite the rain, its white contrasted the darkness. Out of fear and untrust, Abbie shook her head side-to-side and weakly whispered, "*Nonononono!*"

Kayne yanked her hair. "Shut up!"

The woman's hand was never intended for Abbie. Instead, Missus ran her long fingers through Kayne's hair.

"You did get her, didn't you, dear?" Missus said to her son. "I suppose I can let it go this time." She kissed the top of his wet head. "Let's get her inside and you out of the rain."

In the distance, the train station looked farther away to Abbie than ever.

I can't remember, it's been so long.

23

In February of 1978, Eugene Giggins, 19, and Beatrice Giggins, formerly Longenderfer, 18, were newlyweds, but far from being virgins. Bea had been almost a month pregnant with twins when they had tied the knot and when she stood at the altar to be married, no one knew any different. Any glow she had, everyone attributed to the wedding.

Later that year, fraternal twins were born, Kayne and Kaleigh. Bea worked in the library, while Eugene struggled. He was smart, no doubt about it, he just didn't know what he wanted to do. A friend of his, Daryl, said he had landed a job at a company that dealt with freezing people after they died and they were hiring. A newcomer, the company was at least fifteen years or so behind the eight-ball of similar companies. Their niche, as described to Daryl, was they theoretically had a better method of preserving the human body after death. All they needed was their first body to test their theory. Daryl wasn't keen on joining a startup company based on an unproven theory, but joined anyway, wanting to get in on the ground floor of perhaps something big.

Eugene wasn't sure, but he needed the money. After some unusual questions, the company hired him for $8,000 a year. He had a high school diploma and completed some college courses, but never finished. It didn't matter because all they had hired him to do was handle the moving of the dead body throughout the preservation process. Fine with him. Without a body to move yet, money never came easier in his life.

The company's first body, *dead* body to be preserved, came in 1979 and had been processed for free so their theory could be tested. It was the only body received that year, but the company's storage method proved successful as far as anyone knew.

Another corpse came in 1980, where the family paid the full price of storage and perpetual care of $35,000. Expensive for the early eighties, it had been the only body received that year—the concept too new to be widely accepted. Below ground belonged to the dead and storing dead bodies above ground took space from the living.

Two bodies in the company's care in as many years wasn't scoring any runs nor making enough money. With only a body on first and second, the company was on pace to score two years from now. That's if none of the corpses got *out* between now and then. So, rather than paying Eugene only to handle carcasses, the company expanded his role by having him do odd jobs around the facility. Nothing strenuous or complicated, so he gladly did whatever they asked. If anything, the days seemed shorter.

Not everyone at the company rolled with it as Eugene. In fact, other than Daryl, the only place every other employee wanted to roll was out the door to work for another company—preferably one that made money. Constant turnover made it difficult for the company during those initial years. For a while, it appeared the company was about to become stillborn.

However, something had struck Eugene in observing the scientists during those two procedures he had witnessed—*Maybe I can do that?*

Believing he could, he worked at the facility while pursuing a Biology degree, banging out assignments at work when things were slow and banging Bea at home to relieve the stress.

In 1984, Eugene earned a B.S. in Biology. The night he received it in the mail, Bea was anxious to see what he had learned. When she undressed him in haste, her hubby's body was inked from his neck to his toes. "Loan language," he explained before she asked. Of course, the ink was not really there.

Despite owing more than he owned, he immediately enrolled in the Master's program. Debt up to his eyeballs, that was all he saw when he looked through his eyes. Constant reminders kept how much he owed at the forefront of his brain. Principal payments came due more often than he shit. Interest payments every time he pissed. Divorcing Bea so she wouldn't be liable if anything happened to him had crossed his mind, but he was too busy to act on it. Too busy learning.

Meanwhile, scientists came and went from the company so often that the front entrance had been replaced by a revolving door to keep up with a turnover rate of nearly one hundred percent. Rumors floated around as to how the company had paid for it; probably had to borrow. Hell, Eugene could have filled out the paperwork for them.

But through it all, Eugene Giggins had stayed the course at the company, along with his friend, Daryl, learning the ins-and-outs of the science behind human preservation.

More cadavers came in—they weren't going anywhere—as did more money. Business picking up, a promotion was offered to Eugene in taking on scientist duties, doubling his salary to $20,000 a year, as long as he promised to finish his Master's degree. From a company perspective, what's the worst that could happen? It's not like Eugene could kill a cadaver.

Although the $20,000 was well below what other scientists had made, he accepted and went on to receive his Master's. In having the education and on the job experience, who knew for sure whether Eugene would stay or bolt like the rest. Goddamn, those loans.

That summer of 1984, Eugene and Bea bought a brand new 1984 Chrysler Fifth Avenue for a dollar short of twelve grand. How the hell the financing was approved, Eugene never figured, owing as much as he did. But times, salaries, and accepted debt was different back then.

Over time, the company threw more money his way. The degree and experience were important, but above all else, his loyalty to the company warranted a better living. It wasn't long before the Giggins were house-shopping and settled on the property where they currently live.

All of their business dealings had been done using their given names, Eugene and Beatrice Giggins: jobs, taxes, bank accounts, mail, paying those damn P&I payments. But hating their names, they adopted Hugh and Nora.

Now, before thinking them crazy, consider everything a name entailed. This was one of those times when everything could be narrowed down to one thing: *history*. All names have a history particular to them. Not that every Eugene experienced the same one, but *each* Eugene had their own. Of course, the Eugenes with histories worth remembering don't ever think of starting completely over with a clean slate as someone else. On the other hand, histories that need constant fuzzing from drinking, drugs, and debauchery become candidates for drastic change by resetting life as someone else.

It may or may not work, but what the hell. Daily addressing themselves by their *chosen* names, even when friends were around, the names stuck. Daryl started calling Eugene Hugh and Bea Nora without any thought. People do it all the time—a guy named Ed wants to be called Jim. Even accepted nicknames of names don't make sense, like calling someone Dick when their name is Richard. Why not Rich as some do? Who wouldn't want to be called Rich?

October of 1984, Eugene, unofficially going by the name Hugh, and Bea, informally Nora, dropped off their children, Kayne and Kaleigh, both six, at Daryl's house, so Daryl's wife could watch them, while Hugh and Nora went to a Halloween party. They dressed up as Gomez and Morticia Addams from the Addams Family.

After consuming a number of the on-the-house drinks, they had left the party early, wanting to pick up the kids, get home, and put them to bed so they could go to bed themselves and mess around. Messing around first and then getting the kids would have worked, too, but neither of them wanted to head back out after.

After arriving at Daryl's, instead of leaving right away, they stayed and had a few drinks while they talked. A cold drizzle fell that night as the Giggins said their goodbyes and piled into the car.

On their way home, the car sped down a curvy back road. Impaired, Hugh lost control of the car around a 30 mph turn, taking it at a speed-demon 60. The tail of the large car swung into a skid. Panicked, Hugh slammed on the brakes, squealing the tires, leaving skid marks on the road. Smoke formed and spread under the vehicle from the tires rubbing the macadam. Parallel to the street, the car finally stopped; its momentum bore down on the passenger side tires, causing the driver's side wheels to leave the ground.

Maybe Hugh and Nora had forgotten, were in a hurry to get home and mess around, or were drunker than they had thought, but, for whatever reason, the kids were in their backless booster seats but never strapped in before leaving Daryl's.

So, Kaleigh and all forty-two pounds of her had gone airborne across the back seat; her backless booster not far behind. Her head cracked into Kayne's, and then her body slammed into her brother's forty-seven pounds; the booster hit her body. Kayne's body collapsed between the force of Kaleigh's body plowing into him and the car door. His neck jerked violently as the side of his head impacted against the window, fragmenting the glass but not breaking through.

When the driver's side tires had left the ground, it had raised Kaleigh into the air. She slid off her brother at an angle toward the door, but her head hit hard against the bottom of the cracked window, shattering it, spraying glass. Insult to injury, the booster seat hit the back of her head.

Suspended on two wheels, the car couldn't decide on whether it wanted to flip over or stay upright. Either way, gravity would have its way. And it did, pulling the driver's side of the car down on the road. The impact sprung Hugh and Nora off their seats, the top of their heads hitting the roof, while Kaleigh flopped, cracking heads again with Kayne, who remained in his booster seat, which had only shifted underneath him. The car bounced a couple of times until settling to a motionless state, cockeyed in the middle of the road.

The sudden and swift motions caused Nora to roll down her window and puke. Hugh pulled on his door handle numerous times, desperate to get out. For some reason, the lever didn't work, but then the door swung open. Before he got out, warm vomit spewed out of his mouth, splashing against the glistening pavement, producing steam.

Nora got out of the car, screaming.

Hugh opened the driver's side back door and plopped on the backseat where Kaleigh's booster used to be. Carefully yet quickly, he reached for Kaleigh and pulled her motionless body back toward him. Crumbs of glass sprinkled her hair and stuck to the blood on her head. Holding her limp body while backing himself out of the car, he gently laid his daughter down on the back seat.

It began to rain harder. Nora's face looked up at the

night sky. Beads of water pimpled her face. "Why, God? Why?" Nora repeated in different voices as if every octave wanted a turn in expressing her pain.

Hugh went around the car to the other side. Glass chips from the back window crunched under his dress shoes as he, cautiously, opened Kayne's door, ensuring his son didn't tip over and fall out. Blood matted Kayne's hair to his head and glass covered him like glitter. A trail of blood ran from the corner of the boy's mouth down his chin.

While holding Kayne upright, he pulled the backless booster seat out from under him and placed it on the floor with Kaleigh's. After brushing the glass off the back seat, he laid his son's sagging body down next to his sister's. Once the door was closed, he looked at his questioning wife and said, "Shut-up and get in the car."

One final inquiry, refusing not to be heard, "Why, God? Why?", launched through the rainy night toward the heavens. How far it got, no one knows. It's been her experience not much farther than past her mouth.

Only hearing Hugh's door shut and nothing from God, Nora slouched in the rain as if each drop weighed on her head and shoulders. Pummeled by the downpour and not caring, she stood in the middle of the road in contemplation. What, exactly, only she knew. A call out the passenger side open window for her to get her ass in the car did not phase her in the least. Still, she obeyed and sat there in silence with the window open.

The car turned over numerous times but wouldn't start. Headlights appeared from around the bend and grew as a pick-up truck barreled toward the Chrysler, illuminating the falling rain just outside Nora's open window.

Not that Nora cared; there was no reaction.

Attempts by Hugh to start the car had probably flooded the engine. The lights behind his wife's head were large and bright. Raindrops made it almost artistic. Then, he witnessed his wife lose it. Nora turned toward the oncoming vehicle and begged for it to come.

"That's it, you son-and-daughter-of-the-bitchiest-of-bitches! Take your revenge! Smash my brains in and crush my heart under your wheels!"

Hugh pulled the lever in his door, but it stuck as it had before. While his wife begged to die, his cry opposed it—*nononono!*

Huge, bright lights came in through Nora's open window. Hugh's eyes closed tight as he prepared for impact. Nora's eyes bulged, but not in fear, rather in anticipation, watching the hunk of metal coming to *smash her brains in and crush her heart under its wheels.* "Oh, it's like you to answer that one!" she cried out to God.

Those sun-like lights moved off them as the pick-up veered to miss the Chrysler, leaving the Giggins in the dark. There wasn't much room to get by, but enough, as the truck tilted on its chassis, creaking like a boat on the water, attempting a sharp turn.

Watching the truck veer back into its appropriate lane and speed down the road, Hugh whispered, "Fucking asshole!"

He turned to check on Nora and her outstretched fingers nearly poked him in the eye. *"Jesus!"*

Desperately, she reached for the truck like an ailing person hoping to touch Jesus' garment, except, instead of being healed and carrying on, her healing would come in death, where ailments no longer reach—*no more death, sorrow, crying, or pain* type of thing.

Hugh knew his wife. And he also knew she had

somehow found God and lost him in a matter of seconds. More importantly, the car needed to be started and moved before another vehicle barreled down the road—God forbid something larger.

Finally, the car started and Hugh drove his family back to Daryl's house. The entire trip, Nora repeatedly asked in her mind, *Why, God? Why?* Peeking over at his wife, Hugh saw her lips moving without sound.

Arriving at Daryl's, Nora went into the house and stayed there so Daryl's wife could watch her, while Daryl and Hugh transferred the kids into Daryl's car. Hugh insisted on driving, so Daryl tossed him the keys and Hugh drove them and the kids to the facility where they work.

Hugh's demeanor on the outside appeared calm, but inside he wasn't right.

"We have to preserve them!" he said. "They deserve a second chance!"

Daryl tried to console him. "We will, buddy."

"We have to preserve them!"

"We'll take good care of 'em."

"We have to preserve them!"

Daryl started to respond again, but didn't, realizing Hugh's mind skipped like a record in a repetitive funk, stuck there until the act was accomplished.

At the facility, Hugh and Daryl each carried a child into the building, all four of them drenched by the cold rain.

Inside, the kids were undressed, cleaned up, and laid in rolling plastic bathtubs. Hugh started gathering what they needed for the procedure.

Daryl had to ask. "Hey, Hugh. I know this is more than hard, but who checked the kids. I mean, are they dead?"

"We have to preserve them!"

"Hey—Hugh!" Daryl snapped his fingers. *"Come on! Snap out of it, buddy! This is our asses!"*

"They'll live again." Hugh nodded. "Yeah. It'll be alright."

Seeing Hugh's eyes were vacant, Daryl said, "Yeah, okay," and helped Hugh.

Drugs were injected into the six-year-olds. Machines provided compressions, keeping their blood circulating through their bodies. Oxygen masks placed over their mouths and noses kept oxygen moving to the brain.

Looking at their head wounds, Daryl hoped they were neurologically alright to be preserved. Surgery, performed on both thighs of each child, exposed the femoral artery in the right leg where the anti-icing solution entered the body through a tube, while the children's blood drained out of the femoral vein in the left leg. Their bodies were cooled quickly until vitrified, then lowered into a metal container filled with freezing cold gas and sealed up.

Hugh and Daryl cleaned up the scene as they had done with other procedures, working through the night until morning, leaving no evidence as to what they had done.

Daryl demanded his car keys back and drove Hugh to his house to pick up Nora. He let Hugh use his second car to drive Nora home, leaving Hugh's damaged car at his place.

At home, Hugh and Nora came up with a plan. Wearing gloves and accounting for all precautions, they broke into their own home, making it look like a home invasion. The kids' beds were messed up to make it seem as if they had been snatched during their slumber.

They got out of their costumes and cleaned

themselves up.

Looking at herself in the mirror, Nora went to unclasp the chain around her neck and stopped, placing her long fingers over the pendant, deciding to leave it on. She slipped into her pajamas and tucked the pendant inside her top.

The pocket watch rested on the dresser, as Hugh pulled up his pajama bottoms. A strange lure tempted him to put the watch in his pocket—pajama pocket—but he didn't. Who wears a pocket watch when they go to bed? But, later that day, when he had changed for the day, he put it in his pocket.

Since that fateful night, Hugh and Nora have remained in costume—Nora in her pendant and Hugh with his pocketwatch—unable to be themselves, never wanting to return to who they once were, because those people killed their children. Killing Eugene and Beatrice Giggins, the Giggins unofficially became the Thummels.

Some histories aren't worth remembering.

That morning, waiting until the time they typically awake, Nora called the police. Hysterical, she reported a break-in and that her children were missing. During the call, her pain genuinely wished the kids truly had been abducted, so a chance existed they might be alive.

The police came out to the house to investigate. After, they encouraged the Thummels to continue their routines as much as possible and to report any suspicious activity.

Hugh was supposed to work the weekend, but, despite the officer's suggestion, he didn't go in on Saturday. Under the circumstance, Hugh's boss told him to take all the time he needed and not to worry; they'll find the kids.

Hugh hoped not. There would be a lot of explaining to do. Besides, being around canisters filled with frozen people, two of whom his own children, probably wasn't the best medicine.

Little did he know at the time, this closeness became something he would covet later. The dead anywhere else, in the ground, sea, or especially cremated, had zero chance of coming back. Normal and themselves, that is. Not zombies. But not here. This place fanned a flame of hope that the loved ones suspended here may someday live again.

And yet, with the challenges of re-animation pointing and laughing at those who worked here, no one in their right mind could ignore the possibility that all of this effort was nothing more than ass-gas fanned by the blower's waving hand trying to make something out of nothing.

Despite his boss's offer, Hugh returned to work the next day. After work, he returned Daryl's car, then took his own to someone who had agreed to clean it inside and out for a fee, a separate *privacy fee* the dude had called it, and a favor—no refusals.

Holy mothers of all the lesser gods, Hugh hoped this guy forgets this whole thing and never comes cashing in on that favor. Open-ended as it was made him uncomfortable, but who else had the equipment and know-how on lifting blood out of car seats? All hope ended when the guy pulled out a tape recorder, spoke the agreement into it, and then held it near Hugh's face, having him state his full name, social security number, address, phone number, address of where he worked, work number, his wife's full name, her social security number if he knew it, and the names of his kids—not knowing it was their blood he was about to clean up.

It was P&I loan payments all over again.

Having everything he needed, the man made a disclosure threat: *'If I find out that you lied about anything and I can't find you at any time during my lifetime…,'* waited for any admittance or corrections, and then—only then—proceeded with the job.

After, the guy told Hugh he knew a guy who would take care of that window for him, but Hugh passed, not interested in owing another favor.

Instead, Hugh took the car to a regular shop and had the right back passenger window fixed.

Monday morning came and Hugh told his boss he had preserved his children at the facility, purposefully leaving Daryl out of it and all of the details concerning driving under the influence, the accident, the cover-up, and why he waited to tell him.

The boss had a difficult time holding back his great fortune at the expense of Hugh's misfortune. He told Hugh although the loss of his two children seemed permanent, it might not be, they might have a chance to live again and his contributions to science affected all who wanted the same opportunity.

Nothing new to Hugh; it was why he had brought them to the facility in the first place.

Not having any children being preserved before Hugh's, the boss waived the membership fees and paid Hugh a $20,000 bonus, $10,000 for each kid.

A wrinkle in this arrangement came when Mrs. Thummel wanted the children to sleep in their home, preferably as close to their bedrooms as possible, instead of at the facility with the *others*, which had become a derogatory term whenever she mentioned it. Her two kids deserved better and *better* was with her at the house.

The boss conditionally agreed, as long as the arrangement didn't hinder the company from fulfilling its duty of perpetual care. No worries there. The company still had the children in their charge, with Hugh monitoring them nearly around the clock. This was better than keeping them at the facility.

And touching, let's not forget that. *Parents bring dead children home to be close to them.* Headlines don't get any better than that.

The Thummels hired a construction crew to come to the house. Hugh's boss instructed Hugh to tell the contractor how valued an employee Hugh was of the company and, with the abduction of their children and the controversial nature of Hugh's job, wanted a space built out for a panic room somewhere in the house.

The construction workers located a natural dead-spot in the house, a vacant column between the kids' rooms extending from the second-floor ceiling down to over the stairs leading to the basement. Hugh provided dimensions and weight requirements to the contractor, who wanted to work directly with the panic room installers, but was told the information supplied would have to do.

Work began on strengthening the base of the area above the basement stairs for all the electrical wiring and workings of a panic room, including a crawl space with removable panels for access in case of repairs or upgrades. The dead-space, itself, had also been boxed out and strengthened to hold the room. Built-in bookshelves in each of the kids' bedrooms acted as concealed doors, allowing two entrances for access. A third opening, created in the attic floor above the dead-space, allowed for a fourth opening—the roof—to be opened upon delivery of the panic room so that a crane could lower it through the roof and attic floor into the fortified dead-space.

When the build-out work was completed, Mr. Thummel surprised the contractor by paying the sizable balance in cash—compliments of the company.

Of course, a panic room specialist was never hired and a panic room never installed.

Instead, a container used for preserving bodies from Hugh's work had been delivered to the house and cut into six equal sections across the barrel, which made it more manageable, bringing it into the house without further disrupting the Thummels' home.

With a section of the roof removed, the bottom of the container was placed inside the dead-space first, followed by the next section, which was welded to the bottom by a welder inside the tank, and so on until all six sections had been welded together, making a complete container again. Muscular guys with some rope lifted the welder out of the top and through the opening created in the attic floor. Once the inside of the cylinder had been cleaned and fumigated, thoroughly, it would be time for the children.

The container ready, Hugh and Daryl transported the children from the facility to the house. Carefully taken up to the attic, the kids were lowered through the opening in the attic floor into their new container; Kayne's body stored to the side near his bedroom and Kaleigh's near her room. Next came the lid, enclosing the metal casket, and that all-important preserving gas.

The canister holds up to four people; the two children up top and two vacant spaces below. It surprised the Thummels to learn that the other two spots weren't automatically designated for them. The thought of two strangers being stored inside the barrel with her two sleeping babies worried Mrs. Thummel beyond end. How did this happen? This was worse than storing them at the facility where they would each have had their own tank.

Possibly, it might have been a way for the company to claim part of the Thummels' home as a satellite office. Another possibility was forcing the Thummels into paying for the two spots in the container when they pass. Because of Hugh's contributions to the company, instead of using the employee discount of fifty-percent off, the boss gave the two spots to him for free—sort of.

It didn't cost Hugh anything out of pocket. All the boss asked was for the deed to the house to be bequeathed to the company after the last remaining survivor. In doing the math, this equated to less than a fifty-percent employee discount because the home was now worth a tad over $100,000.

But something more elementary than basic math had sealed the deal. Unless re-animation became a reality to where the family could monitor and take care of their own when they were all dead, who would take care of them? It could get tricky. So, Hugh agreed.

In the end, a pleased Mrs. Thummel thought highly of Hugh's company. The children were home and near their rooms. Her and Hugh were set to be preserved with them when their times came. And the house went to the company, providing a valuable service. If the home turned into another facility for storing bodies, that was okay, as long as it happened *after* she was gone *and* their tank remained where it was—at the heart of the house.

Hugh's boss craftily hinted to Hugh that he could earn additional bonuses by bringing more children into the facility, especially an infant. *"It's important that people know preservation isn't just for adults, but everyone,"* he said.

Hugh didn't care for the insinuation.

Every year since 1984, the Giggins morphed into the Thummels, Eugene into Hugh, Bea into Nora, killing the old man and woman over the years and putting on the new every day; her in her pendant and him with his pocket watch.

Most days, Mr. Thummel only traveled between work and home, with the occasional stop at Daryl's for a beer or something stronger. Mrs. Thummel had arranged things so she never had to leave the house, having nearly everything delivered, even groceries.

Over the years, a lot has changed—including Mrs. Thummel's eyes. The pigment in her irises had transformed from green to red shortly after the accident. She never knew why or why Hugh's are still the same, but perhaps, it's because he leaves the house for work and she doesn't. The only answer that ever seemed reasonable was if the eyes were indeed the window to the soul, then the color of her eyes changed to match her new soul—Nora's.

24

Two state police officers had been dispatched out of Station Flat to 513 Spooky Nook Road—but not in Station Knoll—because the address of 513 Spooky Nook Road in Station Knoll doesn't exist. 513 Spooky Nook Road was in the next town over in Station Glen, about twelve miles east of Station Knoll. Officers have been dispatched there numerous times before and knew the exact location.

As the squad car pulled up along the curb in front of the house, a sense of *déjà vu* that this was going to be a complete waste of time dispirited the two officers who had been dispatched there before. With *here we go again* looks on their faces, they sat in the car.

Finally, the Sergeant said to the Corporal, "Stay on your toes. We got a job to do," and they exited the vehicle.

Being safe than sorry, the officers fulfilled their duty by searching the property and the perimeter of the home, already knowing which windows to look through for a scan inside. As usual, there was nothing to see and nothing to report. The place had been abandoned since 2000.

Since 1985, the police have visited 513 Spooky Nook Road in Station Glen at least once a year. During those early years, people moved in and out of that address like a hotel room, never there long enough to grow tired of the police visits. If the same person answered the door that was there for the last visit by the coppers, it was always a huge surprise.

In 1995, after a decade of rumors, the place had gained a stigma of being haunted. For this reason, a psychic bought the property dirt-cheap. But after a year of no inexplicable phenomena, the physic moved out and put the home on the market. After two years, multiple price reductions, and only one nibble—not a serious one at that—where numerous attempts by the psychic to reach inside the mind of the nibbler to increase her appetite for the place had failed, he sold it to Station Glen for a dollar.

The loss was worth getting rid of the place. Why Station Glen hadn't offered to buy it two years ago was beyond him. They could have saved him time, effort, and money, but what the hell—it was out of his thinning hair now. A colossal mistake in buying it, wisdom countered with, *One must learn from one's boneheadedness by using the bone to beat the stupidity out of oneself.*

Finalizing the transaction was the last time anyone had seen the psychic and, after receiving his dollar, the last anyone had heard was when he had stormed out of the building, mentioning something about heading for New Jersey.

Town hall meetings used to have the property on the agenda to discuss its potential uses, until people got tired of talking about it. Every now and again, some brave soul resurrects it, only to be silenced by avoidance and inaction.

Electronically, Abbie's picture, along with Mrs. Syfert's description of Nora Thummel and the *all-black* car, had reached all in-state precincts and select ones out-of-state. Not having the year, make, and model of the vehicle was problematic. More than that—down-right dung. Problems could be systematically solved. But that takes time; time authorities didn't have. Besides, with the 513 address a bust, where do they begin? It would take someone knowing the situation, seeing Abbie, Nora Thummel, or an all-black vehicle, and then having the cojones to call it in. It might be asking for a miracle, but, at this point, that's what they needed.

State police searched the names of Hugh and Nora Thummel in the state and crapped out a single turd, as in a big, fat zero. No one with those names or variations lived in the state. And when select police departments in surrounding states performed their own searches, a few names spewed out, but they were deceased.

Without having their middle names, initials, or other pertinent information, such as their dates-of-birth or social security numbers, there was no way of narrowing the search for better results.

In researching the newspaper ad, who placed it and paid for it, they thought they were in business. Until the name and information were found to be fictitious. The only connection made was that similar ads had been placed the last three years during the same month but under a different name and information each time, of course, fabricated. Record retention at the newspaper only went back three years and with these particular ads paid-in-full, up-front, and in cash, there were no red flags.

Even the phone number in the ad was one of those one-and-done numbers. Once the *unfortunate soul* called for the sitting job, the number and identification of anyone associated with it were dry leaves in October's wind, already crumbling and disintegrating into oblivion. As obscure as scam and spam callers, invading your home through your phone while remaining undetectable and untraceable. Fucking cowards!

Running out of options, probably the best chance of pinpointing Abbie's location was by tracking her cell phone number, but so far, the police were yet to get a signal.

All I know is now and *now* is awful.

25

Not a soul in sight. Not a soul in earshot. A steady rain slapped the muddy cornfields—*cornfields galore*—around the Thummels' place. Raindrops detached leaves from trees and brought them to the ground. Even leaves returned to the dust when it was their time.

The time—November 1, Allhallows, the day after Halloween.

All anyone has is *now*. And that went for Abbie. Whose *now* was awful! Not many on Earth had the Halloween she had. Nor the Allhallows she's having *now*.

Do I choose my life's path, or does fate decide for me? she had pondered once. A lifetime ago, it seemed. Yet, it had only been a week. That's all it took to figure it out. Fate chose for her because she wouldn't have chosen this shit for herself. Who would? A masochist, maybe.

In a quirky rhythm, the rain beat on the Thummels' roof as a bongo player might during a ritual, either to Satan or to a god with a unique power and an exotic-sounding name, such as *Doof—the god of the all-you-can-eat buffet.*

Strapped down to Kaleigh's bed, Abbie struggled to free her wrists and ankles. The lights were off. Some time ago, Kaleigh, inside Mrs. Thummel, had explained to her that *'girls sleep in her room and boys sleep in Kayne's room.'* Watching and hearing a child's voice come out of an adult's mouth had caused Abbie to blurt out, "What the fuck is happening?" followed by a painful moan of "Oh, God!"

There was no getting used to something as bizarre as that, no matter how many times she had witnessed it. And although they were appropriate responses under the circumstances, Mrs. Thummel had slapped Abbie's mouth forehand and backhand for interrupting her daughter then left the room.

A deep thinker like Abbie took Kaleigh's words literally and wondered, *How many kids have slept here? How many are still sleeping?*

Exhausted, wet, and muddy, all she wanted was to be free, go back in time and undo everything. Yes, before Halloween night. Back before her father's death, which would mean Oliver would be alive, too. Escaping the *now* mattered most. Then, maybe, she could sleep. With everything right in the world, sure she could. The Thummels wanted her to sleep, too—*forever.*

Someone entered the bedroom. When the black

silhouette got into Abbie's view, long hair, dangling from the head, positively identified the someone as Mrs. Thummel. For no matter who was at the controls, Missus or Kaleigh, there was no mistaking Missus' body.

Ignoring Abbie, the woman fiddled with things, knickknacks and such, straightening them, from Abbie's tantrum earlier when Mister had manhandled her into the bedroom and tied her down to the bed.

Her work took her out of Abbie's view, then, all of a sudden, Missus bent over the bed, looking down at Abbie. Frizzed, crusted hair, wet-dried and dark, hung down like leafless trees, crooked and gnarled, in a spooky forest. Those red eyes peeked out from behind, looking more maroon, blood-filled, warning it's not safe to enter the woods.

"I see we're still fighting, dear," Mrs. Thummel said.

Ah, it was Missus. Fear stretched Abbie's eyes round; the rope rubbed anew on the reddened rawness around her wrists and ankles as she fought to free herself; her neck strained in defiance as she demanded, "Let me GO!"

"I'm afraid we can't do that, darling. We're a family, the four of us, and families stick together."

"I don't know what you're on, you crazy bitch, but you better let me go." Hysterical, mad, Abbie violently screamed, "YOU CRAZY BITCH! LET ME GO!"

Those red eyes looking out from behind the trees intensified in color, brightened near fluorescent, from Missus becoming angry, challenged by Abbie's outbursts.

Like a deer mesmerized by headlights, Abbie stared into them, wondering how they could do that, and why they were no longer pale-red. It wouldn't be a car grille, but she expected to be hit all the same. Probably, the same forehand-backhand combination that had been the go-to method of punishment. Why not? It worked before.

Gradually, Missus' eyes dimmed, returning to a darker maroon. An unfazed demeanor of calm graced the woman's movements when she stood up and walked toward the window.

No doubt, Mrs. Thummel was here in entirety: both body and spirit. It wasn't farfetched to believe that Kaleigh still wandered around in there, waiting for her turn.

A new paranoia bounced Abbie's eyeballs to the farthest reaches of the room. Something more troubling than the daughter in her mother opened Abbie's mind to another possibility. One that needed serious consideration. Because if it occurred, Abbie doubted she could survive it. And that was maybe Kaleigh wasn't inside her mother anymore. Was it possible the young girl was loose in the room? On her way toward Abbie? To harm her—or worse—*enter* her?

"*Nooo! Nooooo!*"

Long moans leaked out of Abbie, while her wide eyes scanned the air of the room, fully expecting to see something moving within it. What exactly, she didn't know. But something.

Moonlight passed through the window and caressed Missus' face. Not like a lover, but more like a father, who failed to have a son. Night's daughter, heir to nighttime, moonless or moonlit, it would someday, rightfully, belong to her.

"Kayne's helping his father get things ready in the basement," Mrs. Thummel said, looking out the window with an aura of moonlight, blurring the contours of her beaming face. "Oh, how he loves to help his father. It's their special time together."

The blurring on Missus' face made Abbie wonder if Kaleigh was still inside her mother. Oh, how she wished—

A recharged Missus turned around with a sudden burst of energy, crusted hair swinging across her face before settling straight. A flicker of illumination appeared in her red eyes, much like light hitting a red reflector on a bike.

But no light hit them, not now, because she faced *into* the bedroom with her back to the window. Whatever powered her eyes came from within, just as when she had bent over the bed to look down at Abbie. Somehow, someway, she had drawn power from the sun, reflecting off the moon. And as soon as Abbie thought maybe she was seeing things, that tricks on her eyes continued past Halloween into Allhallows, Mrs. Thummel's eyes dimmed down to normal again.

Normal. Another useless word, worse than *maybe.* It's incorrectly used all the time as in *right and wrong* when really it's a trend. And what was normal for the Thummels was far from the norms Abbie was used to. A clear deviation. *Abnormal* would describe her night— and the Thummels.

"Before you go to sleep, dear, would you like to hear a bedtime story?"

There was nothing more for Abbie to do or say. Everything tonight had moved her further away from a reality she didn't fully understand. How her life had gone so far left her with many questions, but she could operate in that existence. Not this. This was another realm more foreign than any place on Earth she had never been. Overcoming language barriers, abiding by customs, and all of that other international stuff wasn't going to happen because she didn't want any part of it.

As Abbie turned her head away from the direction of Mrs. Thummel not to see her anymore, tears rolled from her top eye, over the bridge of her nose, into her lower eye—also shedding tears—and doubly down her cheek. A tear waterfall, carrying everything from all of Abbie's time on Earth. Short time. No one could see *everything* within the tears, even under a microscope, but they were there. Smaller than *yoctos* but powerful enough to inflict pain. Blame everything: an unfortunate past, a perilous present, and the void of no future, for them being there among the other ingredients that made those tears her's. Fuller tears, welled and swelled with lots and lots of bad.

She had *then*, but that passed, yet still with her. Never had a *future*, no one does, until they get there, but then it becomes *now*. That's where she was. All she had was *now*. And *now* was awful.

So much so, a lot of tears secreted from a dreadful realization: she didn't know the way back to that prior reality. As bad as it was, it was better than *now*. Her mom was there. Hope was there. And life. *Here* and *now*, she was alone, without hope, and may die.

How long will they drag this out? Before sunrise—that's not long? How? How will I die?

That kind of thought wasn't meant for a teenaged girl. Thoughts of the future: where to go to college, who she might marry—those kinds of things would come now and again. Practical things, like grades and chores, too. But boys, what to wear to the dance, or on a date, a particular boy, is he going to ask me out, should I go to this party, drink, smoke, snort, how far am I willing to go with him—all should be the stuff on a normal girl's mind. Not this shit.

But this wasn't normal. Maybe that made Abbie abnormal, too. Guilty by association.

One thing was for sure: Missus wasn't normal. Not by anyone's standard, whether they had one or not. Proven by her telling Abbie a bedtime story.

26

Put to bed to sleep forever, Abbie laid and listened to the *bedtime* story. Not facing Mrs. Thummel, she didn't see that the cracked nut—cracked in the ass, cracked in the crotch, talking through a crack in her face, and, apparently, cracked in the head—had once more brightened those fluorescent red eyes, stimulated by the story, glowing like a toxic leak from missus' unstable nuclear reactor of a brain. Strange how a story could power such a thing. Then again, not that strange. Good stories always had the power to provoke.

"I always wanted children, dear," Missus blabbed out of the crack in her face. "*Eventually,* you see, just not at eighteen. I was so thrilled when Kayne and Kaleigh were born. But from then on, it seemed life sped toward me. At times, I sped through life. And just when I thought life couldn't go any faster, we sped toward each other.

"The responsibility and learning took over my life. There was no time for anything else. We didn't know parenting was going to be so hard. We talked about putting them up for adoption, but we couldn't. Adoption would put us too much in control—and we didn't want that. No, it had to be natural. God's will."

God? This woman?

Abbie couldn't believe what she was hearing. Slightly, she turned toward her, but not far enough to see her.

"For almost five years, I prayed to God to take them away. He never did." Missus' voice lowered. "Looking back, he never answered one prayer."

God, again, Abbie thought.

Missus said no more. Perhaps, the crack had been calked or cracked all the way. Paranoid, Abbie's eyeballs moved side-to-side in their sockets as she wondered, *What's happening. Why is she quiet? What is she up to? Did she think I fell asleep? Is she getting ready to kill me? How?*

Her sixth sense kicked in. Something was wrong. The nut must have moved—closer. The air had changed. Hair, great and small, short and tall, raised all over her body. All senses peaked now. Her eyeballs ticked-tocked faster back and forth. Warm pee twinkled onto her underwear and showed through the pants. It wasn't much, but enough. Not having anything to eat or drink for a long time, it smelled terrible. It had to be yellow, she knew, dark yellow. Her skin squirmed on her flesh, cowering perhaps, knowing what was coming before she did.

Abbie whipped her head around so she knew, too. Somethings were better unknown. Overloaded as if being electrocuted, her limbs straightened and body locked rigid, tensed under intense pressure. Every hole in her head expanded: eyes wide, nosed raised with nostrils exposed, mouth agape, ears sensitive to her own screaming. What she witnessed was blasphemous. Unexplainable. Revolting. Everything evil in one.

Apart from the glowing red eyes, Kaleigh's young facial features had merged behind her mother's: four eyes, two noses, and two mouths comingled lenticular on one face, a face overlaying another face, each entity separate from the other. The young girl looked out of her mother as casually as looking out a window—like mother, like daughter.

When Kaleigh's features pressed forward, skin and bones on her mother's face protruded out, similar to seeing an expecting mother's belly bulge from her baby's foot pressing against it when it kicked. The girl's face moved forward, increasing in size, aligning her features with her mother's.

Mrs. Thummel's mouth moved, speaking in Kaleigh's voice. "Yes, Mommy! I like this story."

What was there to like? Only something damned would find this story likable.

Out of Abbie's agape mouth, a delayed caterwaul blared. Not exactly a sound she wanted to hear while looking at that abomination. It only exacerbated her fear, too fitting with what she saw. A scream as before would have been better. At least it would have sounded human instead of animalistic.

In her own, adult voice, Mrs. Thummel continued with the story over Abbie's howling. "It was hard on your mother. I gave God a chance, darling, more than one. Then, one day…"

"It was hard on Mommy," Kaleigh's voice

interjected—out of her mother's mouth—listening intently to her mother.

They were both here: mother and daughter together—factually—the dead inside the living—sharing the same face. Mrs. Thummel would have slapped Abbie for such an interruption: forehand, then backhand. But Kaleigh was here, too. Maybe, as long as the girl's presence hung around, Abbie could stay around a little longer.

Abbie's throat hurt, scratchy, rubbed raw by the caterwaul still coming. And she had no control to stop it.

"That's right," mother said, seamlessly, right after her daughter. Despite Abbie's shrilling, she went on. "So, one day, it hit me. I started thinking about alternatives. I gave up on God as he did me. It seemed like every month of that year, Hugh and I tried something new. Religions, spells, witchcraft, the occult. We prayed to anyone, anyone at all…"

Abbie wailed and it sounded more human. To her surprise, *"God—Help me,"* leaked out amid it and she thought, *My left wrist is loosening.*

"…who would answer, vowing to worship who or whatever would answer. It wasn't until…"

"Yes, Mommy."

They're connected, Abbie thought. *Two bodies in the room, yet three of us here.*

There was no way of making the math work.

"…we started Satanic rituals, and, *oh*, dear, we felt different. Things began to happen we couldn't explain. *Answers. Genuine answers.* To prayers we thought were unanswerable. That's when we started worshipping the angel Lucifer."

Satan. Lucifer. As if everything now made sense,

which it didn't, not to Abbie, her wailing ceased, like an opera singer abruptly stop singing on a particular note.

"Splendid," Mrs. Thummel said, grabbing a wooden chair along the wall and carrying it over to the bed.

So this is how? Abbie thought. *Bludgeoned by a chair.*

"Stay away from me!" Abbie said, sounding scratchy through a damaged throat.

It's loose! Hold the rope and bed slat!

Beside the bed, holding the chair, looking down at Abbie with those eyes ablaze, Mrs. Thummel said, "Satan rewards his living followers and punishes them in death," then set the chair down, sat, crossed her legs, and continued.

"Within a year, it happened. Hugh and I were so excited for Halloween. We were invited to a party—a Halloween party—and decided to go. We had a few drinks then left early. Picking up the kids at a friend's house, we had a few more. Nothing outrageous.

"Driving home, it had been raining on-and-off all night, so the roads were slick. Rounding a bend, we entered a skid. Hugh tried controlling the car, but there was some kind of malfunction or something. When he applied the brakes, the possessed car nearly flipped over—with all of us in it."

ShutupShutupShutup! Abbie thought. *The right is loosening.*

"Kayne and Kaleigh were strapped in their seats when their buckles loosened, don't ask me how they just did. Well …" Emotion choked Missus up. "… between the skid and the car slamming back down to the ground …"

Her face reddened. Inflammation around the eyes. Tears blurred the red and whites of her eyeballs.

"… they died."

"It's okay, Mommy," Kaleigh said.

"I know, darling," mother said.

This duality in one person went beyond what Abbie could stand.

Please, God! PLEEEASE hear my prayer.

After wiping tears away from her eyes and off her cheeks, Missus pressed on.

"Initially ... I thought ... *Satan* had answered. That he had ... taken them away. Then, while looking up into the rain, I realized how much I loved them."

She closed her eyes and her head began to sway to music no one else heard but her—maybe Kaleigh.

"Pain and anguish filled me. Worse than the previous five years combined when they were alive. Oh, it was wonderful."

A contented peace made her smile. She remembered her children dying, and she was smiling. Happy.

She doesn't notice, Abbie thought. *Oh, God! WHERE ARE YOU! HELP ME!*

The woman's eyes opened; Abbie wished she had kept them closed.

"Hugh and I weren't to blame. It wasn't our fault. It was no one's fault."

It was how Missus remembered it.

Within Mrs. Thummel's peaceful face, Kaleigh's face pouted. "Mommy was sad."

Mrs. Thummel's long fingers took turns wiping newly-formed tears from under her glowing red eyes; behind them were Kaleigh's blue eyes. Converged in that way, they looked purple.

"Mommy *was* sad," Missus persisted. "I realized what a mistake it was to wish you and Kayne away. Family was all we had—all we'll ever have.

"But, *oh*, I felt wonderful, too. More alive than I had

in a long time."

Mrs. Thummel cleared her voice. "We learned that lesson and vowed never to let anything keep us apart."

Thunder boomed outside and Missus' head snapped in the direction of the window. Lightning cast gray light in through the window onto her face—and through it as if x-rayed, detailing what should have been a young girl's face—but wasn't. All this time, Kaleigh's face behind her mother's had resembled the front part of a human head. Now, it was nothing more than a surface of a thing, not far from whitewashed windows of a storefront with the lights off inside—broad, swirled soap strokes over a black existence.

Lightning flashed on and off as if snapping pictures. In between takes, darkness soaked Missus like a black dye, who sat alone in the chair. But when the flashes occurred, it revealed something else occupied the chair with her—something the moonlight had failed to do.

Unsettled in her chair, Mrs. Thummel rocked forward and back like a mental patient in a psych ward, unsure what to do next. Mumbling ensued. *"Apart. Never. Never again."* Clustered rain splashed against the windowpane as if someone outside had sprayed a water hose past; she rocked faster. *"Never again. Never again. No, never again."*

This was not the same woman. Self-control and her ability to control others had deteriorated as she told her bedtime story.

Perhaps, it wasn't a story at all but a spell. A spell infused with the power to transport her every way but physically back to the night of the accident. Both stories and spells contain words, so why not a *spellbinding story* since words and their associations can conjure up the past quicker than a medium conducting a séance with an Ouija board in a room, having a mirrored ceiling and a hexagram painted on the floor.

With Kaleigh occupying Mrs. Thummel and Missus distracted by lingering ghosts of her past, including the ghost of her daughter, Abbie worked freer and faster on that rope around her left wrist.

27

The lightning stopped flashing. Doom rendered the room the darkest it's been all night. A tickle gently brushed Abbie's vagina and she shivered as if the temperature in the room had dropped, but it didn't. A tiny amount of pee leaked, that was all.

Clouds, moving between the window and the moon, had caused the perceived phenomenon and when they had passed, the moonlight came through the window once more. And on Mrs. Thummel's face. A face no longer distant, uncertain, distracted. The moon had returned Missus to her old self, firm, in control of herself, and everyone in the house.

Confidently, she stood out of the chair, walked over to the bookshelf, and swung it open until it was flush against the wall. Pale, long-fingered hands belonging to Missus emerged in the moonlight like spiders jumping out from their hiding place. They touched the reflective container, hid away inside the house, and caressed it in a loving, almost sensual way.

"My children," she said, "are preserved in here." Slowly, her arms swayed back and forth from stroking the can. "My little darlings. One day, they will live again."

Mrs. Thummel's eyes cherished the can, worshipped it.

The rope around Abbie's left wrist took some finagling, but, finally, it was coming undone. Concentrating, Abbie took her eyes off Missus to look at the rope to see how much farther it had to go. When she turned back, Missus snapped her head around like a startled animal, staring at her. Those red eyes began to glow and intensify like brake lights on a vehicle. They brightened to the point that, despite the dark, Abbie could see the smile on mother's face and, simultaneously, Kaleigh's childish mouth grinning behind it.

Nothing tonight had gone how Abbie had thought it would. A simple sitting job—that was all it was supposed to be. Not this surreal—

Oh, shit! What's she—

Bright-eyed and badass, Mrs. Thummel took a step toward Abbie, wide eyes fixed on the young girl, and proclaimed, "Let them sleep undisturbed."

Then, the crazy woman spun around and moved toward the hollow of the house. "Sealed and preserved," she continued, eyeing the metal cylinder as if it were the ninth wonder of the world. Emerging once more, her pale, long-fingered hand reached out and, upon touching the canister, she said, "In their burial chamber."

Those familiar, spellbinding words tickled Abbie's brain as if something unwanted crawled in it—*pitter-patter, pitter-patter*. The sensation brought on a disoriented, sick feeling, a little like vertigo, a lot like her stomach had dropped, about to empty out of her. Quite contrarian, especially when she was lying down.

But those words, scurrying around in her mind, had found fertile ground in her brain tissue. Familiar, for she had seen them. Read them. And saw them some more. That inhuman *woman-thing* touching something inside the house that didn't belong had recited the first three lines of the poem from memory.

> *Let them sleep undisturbed*
> *Sealed and preserved*
> *In their burial chamber*

Poems and songs were mostly written about blue eyes or green—not red. Nor should poetry be read by a person with red eyes. The demonic don't read poetry.

Mrs. Thummel continued, not reading poetry, but reciting it. Abbie listened—and cried.

> *"Once a year after Halloween night*
> *They live once more through another's might*
> *Inside a bodily container*
> *Come midnight they awake*
> *A soul for a soul to take*
> *The souls in terrible danger*
> *One soul will do if at least twice their age*
> *But the unfortunate soul gets double their rage*
> *Before returning to the chamber."*

Rawness presided over the room and hushed it. The kind only found during births and deaths. Where race, religion, color, creed, or wealth don't matter. When only two types of people suggested any categorization at all: those dead and those alive to remember them.

This mysterious, fine line between the two emitted a faint smell yet deceivingly potent because Abbie tasted it. To her, they reminded her of death because it wasn't something she smelled in life. What else could this new smell be? Several things. However, this was very specific. Living and dying comingle together during everyone's existence. A *dying life* would be more accurate of a description as well as depressing, so *dying* comes off, leaving only *life*.

But this wasn't that. This was the cusp of death, *her's*, so close Abbie smelled it, *and* death itself, historical, not her's yet, but others, and she could taste it.

"For a time," Mrs. Thummel broke in, now presiding over the room, always had. "Hugh and I just lived, not worshiping anything except family. We tried disregarding what was down in the basement, going as far as taking our clothes to a laundromat. But we couldn't. It called to us."

Missus' hand caressed the canister one last time.

"One night," she began, turning around and moving toward Abbie.

"STAY AWAY!" Abbie yelled at the one coming. "Oh, please, God, make her stay away!" she pleaded a longshot to possibly the only one within earshot.

The right's loose. – Hold it! – Hold it!

"...we went down to the basement to see if we could conjure our children's spirits," Missus explained, taking her time walking toward Abbie. "They didn't come. Instead, another spirit had come to us with an offer. Once a year, at midnight, when Halloween becomes All Saint's Day, the kids would come back to life. Hugh and I wanted that very much, so we agreed. The spirit taught us the rules. A soul for a soul. We get the kids for a day if we give a soul for eternity. But, because our kids were each six when they had died, we had to kill two children at least the age of six or one at least the age of twelve."

The raw fragrance and flavor intensified for Abbie. It might have been the confession; it could also be from the possessed killer coming her way. All doubt had vanished. She would die soon. And the story would die with her.

As if Abbie needed more convincing, Missus said, "The first year, we killed a boy, eight years old, and a girl, nine. They were trick-or-treating on their own with no one watching them. Parents can be too trusting. When it was done, we expected our kids would rise from the dead. In our excitement, we removed the lid off the container to see if they had come back to life.

"They were still asleep," she said softly, still disappointed to this day. "So, to keep them preserved, Hugh resealed the top and filled the tank with more gas. We had no clue that they would live through us, Kaleigh in me, and Kayne in Hugh. It's only one day a year, but the closeness, *oh, darling*, it's indescribable. Not knowing what to do…"

Insane mumbling escaped involuntarily out of Abbie's mouth. Utterances void of words, for Mrs. Thummel spoke enough for both of them. Moans were more accurate. Useless sounds. Worse than an infant. No one listening would know she needed saving. Yet, it was more fundamental than feeding, changing, or needing held. How was that possible?

Because God or some other believed savior usually got those types of calls. Abbie had left numerous messages, but God hadn't returned her call.

"…with the bodies," Missus continued. "Hugh

suggested preserving them by giving them to his company. They were accepted, no questions asked. They took the loss and fudged the paperwork. No one would think of opening preservation tanks to ID missing children. A little marketing and the company saw an influx of legitimate clients. So much so they now have a children's wing. All because of Hugh's hard work."

Anticipating her own death had started the dying process prematurely. It made Abbie bananas. Even monkeys know to peel them before eating them. And she was being peeled to be eaten. An unraveling, if you will. The separation of body from spirit. Or a defense mechanism, so when it happened, she wouldn't know what was happening.

"It's a fine line to walk," Missus said, "and a lot of responsibility. Killing one is easier than two and generally less messy. Every town across America has at least one child go missing a year, so as long as we play by the rules and alternate between the towns around us, it's fairly easy to go unnoticed."

Aaagh! You're fucking crazy, lady!

A nearly peeled banana, Abbie barely had the mental wherewithal to think it, let alone say it.

The bedroom not that big, Mrs. Thummel had stood bedside for a while. Her red eyes peered down at Abbie as if she had heard her thought.

"Don't worry, dear," she said flatly. "It will all be over soon. Hugh now has a less messy way of ceasing life."

A long, shiny needle appeared, twinkling between her glowing red eyes.

Beads of sweat dotted Abbie's purple face—dark like a rotting banana, a dying banana—as she turned away then back again as if having a bad dream. And she was. Coarse sounds escaped her mouth. More mumbling. *No*, the only recognizable word.

"*Oh*, come now, dear. Don't be so difficult. It's the best way to go—immediate and painless. A pinprick and you'll be sound asleep."

28

Dabbling in the dark arts all those years ago after the accident, the Thummels had opened a portal in the basement. At the time, that's all they knew—that *it* was in the basement. Where it led to on the other side, they didn't know or care, because all they wanted was an answer and who or what provided it didn't matter.

'We tried disregarding what was down in the basement,' Missus had said earlier. *'But we couldn't. It called to us.'*

Since that time of—*what?* Misunderstanding? Not expecting an answer? Fear? Regret? Wanting to close the gate, but couldn't—not a gateway because the gate couldn't be closed?—Mrs. Thummel, more than Mister, had thought about the other side and who or what had answered. And that's what it was, wasn't it? An answer. For they had called out, their voice signaled over the Earth, down into the Earth, and across the universe. They had hoped for such range. Open-minded. Open-hearted. Open-spirited. That was if they weren't one and the same.

Although they had summoned Satan, specifically, for Missus had said that she and Hugh had *'started Satanic rituals,'* an openness remained. At the time, they didn't have any allegiance to Satan or anyone or anything. That all changed when *'Satan had answered.'*

Whether it was Satan himself or not, they had no way of knowing. Nor does anyone, for that matter. That little voice in the head or audible speech could be anyone or anything—even yourself. Voices heard usually lack a form. Funny how people listen anyway and they have no clue who or what they are communicating with. The Thummels sure didn't. Their focus was on the promise. Not on having to see the dealmaker, which they never did.

Voices also usually speak the listener into action, good or bad, and fail to do anything themselves.

Not this *Satan*, believed in wholeheartedly by the Giggins, who became the Thummels. This thing, angel or otherwise from the other side, displayed power worthy of their praise by offering to *return* their children to them once a year in exchange for another child: *One soul will do if at least twice their age*, or two: *A soul for a soul.* A promise kept since.

Now that was standing on the promises; Hugh, Nora,—and Satan, the keepers of those promises. That was one *hell* of a run. No other player in the game had a string like that going.

But deities, carbon-based lifeforms, ideas, and systems all suffer the same flaw: imperfection. All those times they had conversed and transacted in the basement, Satan had never brought up that the Giggins children *never died in the car accident.*

Maybe Satan had forgotten or was being gracious, especially to Hugh, who had made the command decision to preserve the kids, without making sure the children were dead—as his friend Daryl had suggested.

Neither parent knew what the deity knew, ignorant that it wasn't Kayne's and Kaleigh's time to die. With the children physically, mentally, and emotionally alive at the time of the accident, nothing had triggered their spirits to move on to their final destination—or oblivion, so they remained inside their comatose bodies; each of their bodies and souls paired together, matched, so creation was in balance.

Which also meant they had witnessed the entire preservation procedure, yelling within themselves, unable to communicate with their father or Daryl that they were alive during the extreme lowering of body temperature, draining of the blood, and refilling with solution so that all of their physical parts: bodies, organs, and brains were vitrified, inactive, suspended in time, and, in doing so, they never shut down. Their lives halted, but not stopped. Buried alive, not just upright above ground in a metal coffin, but trapped inside themselves, mummified, not in spices and linen, but flesh and bone preserved in a freezing gas.

Mainly, time and scientific progress would determine whether or not their bodies had a chance of being re-animated successfully, as in entirely, which was the goal. Nothing was more critical to cryonics than the progress of science toward re-animation. Time, on the other hand, was something the Giggins-Thummel children weren't lacking, being preserved longer than they had aged—six years.

Leaving their bodies once a year on Allhallows Day

was a rare treat, especially when they're bottled up within themselves for the other three-hundred and sixty-four days. And every year, the itchiness became more unbearable. Worse, as frozen cadavers, they couldn't scratch.

The math wasn't in their favor, grossly lopsided and worsening exponentially. One day free to roam inside their parents compared to three hundred and sixty-four trapped in the cold. Two days compared to seven hundred and twenty-eight. Three days compared to one thousand and ninety-two. Year ten, those kids had a *nugatory* ten days out of three thousand six hundred and forty in *purgatory*. Now double that. Triple it. One tiny, fatty piece of pork in a can of beans. Bummersville for those canned broods.

Thank *the tank* they're young! Not dumb, just adaptable. At age six, things weren't fully developed to begin with, so Kayne and Kaleigh had adjusted to their limitations. Same environment, essentially, still being inside themselves as they always were, but coping with having to exist mentally, emotionally, and spiritually in that suspended state had taken its toll. What had it been—thirty years? *Thirty days out of ten thousand nine hundred and twenty! A lousy month!* Thirty fatty pieces of pork in that giant-sized can of beans called a preservation tank. No doubt, the giant would bitch. A can of pork and beans should have a reasonable amount of pork in it; otherwise, just put beans on the label and call it what it is.

Thirty days was thirty days, but come on. And when they do leave their benumbed bodies, they're still not free, transitioning out of their own bodies inside the metal canister into their parent's bodies, containers in their own right, still confined—and shared. When they're done having their fun, they transition right back into that can of beans and into the pork—their bodies. Maybe it should be a can of stew because that's what they do in there—*stew*.

Even at age six, the kids had often thought of how they could remove their parents' spirits from their bodies without killing them so they could be the sole operators of such vessels.

Then it had escalated to thoughts on how to kill their parents while inside them, in hopes their parents' spirits, as well as their own, would abandon the flesh and go *anywhere but here*.

Naturally, this elevated to thoughts of evicting their parents so they could have the apartment all to themselves.

As far as possessing someone else other than their parents, well, rule-keeper and believer that the devil is in the details, it wasn't allowed. To do otherwise would break the agreement.

It's a proven fact that six-year-olds can reason such thoughts. These two youngsters, in particular, even more so. Old souls, they were, having all the time in the world and eternity to contemplate, wonder, and fantasize.

Many people feel trapped within themselves or in a particular situation, wanting to be free. Confined to their unanimated bodies and metal cylinder, the Giggins-Thummel children also fancied freedom.

Until then, one thing was for sure. When they leave their cold, stiff bodies for their parent's warm, animated ones, they were ready to play.

29

As Mrs. Thummel hunched over the bed, lowering the syringe, both of Abbie's eyes moved toward their tear ducts, converging on the needle coming toward her. An animalistic instinct of self-preservation surged through her. Primitive, yet it contained an intelligence. Things in her life she didn't understand or in part were now understandable. As complicated as life could be, this situation wasn't complicated. Live or die? Binary with no middle ground. There was no way of existing for long half-dead. Eventually, that state resulted in either life or death.

And Abbie knew this. She understood it, for she had experienced this through the passing of her father and then Oliver without having to die herself. Death was done, no more—the body extinct. Irrelevant of beliefs or religious practices, nearly everyone on Earth eventually discarded the body by burying it, burning it, studying it somewhere remote, and, yes, even canning it.

Do we choose our life's path, or does fate choose for us? Abbie had thought not long ago and thought now, for a fleeting moment, that she would soon find out. But instead of discovering which one, she had decided that no one was going to choose for her: fate, Missus, anybody. The choice was hers, and she wanted to live.

Yes. Abbie wanted to live. Without question. Right now. *Right fucking now!* This was her time—her moment. *Let's go!* The fight for life. Fuck that needle. Fuck Missus. And with all that pent-up anger directed at that bitch, Abbie grabbed the insane witch by the wrist, stopping the needle's progress.

A gasp of surprise expelled out of Mrs. Thummel. Rope dangled loosely around both of Abbie's forearms. It had happened so fast that Missus reacted by pounding on Abbie's face and head as hard as she could with her free-hand, yelling, "You little bitch!"

A couple of blows landed, but it could have been worse. For Missus punched and slapped with her weaker, uncoordinated left-hand, so her right could steadily drive-home the needle, which hadn't made any progress since Abbie had grabbed her.

Abbie's left hand let go of the killer's wrist and braced that forearm defensively over her face. While punches and slaps rained down, she tried grabbing the attacking hand, wrist if she could get it, with her own but missed. Another attempt…and another…and…she got it, the wrist.

Stalemated with their arms crisscrossed between them, right versing right and left versing left, each fought for control: Abbie to live, Missus to kill so her kids could go on living.

Having the higher ground, Mrs. Thummel leaned forward and pushed down, using her weight. Supported by the bed, Abbie countered by locking her arms but didn't have the strength to sit up. As their faces turned darker shades and their arms shook from the struggle, creaks and squeals sounded from the bed, burdened by the opposing forces.

Life didn't get much rawer than this. One-on-one. *Mano-a-mano.* In a second-floor bedroom of a house surrounded by cornfields galore. No one in sight. No one in earshot. No one coming to the rescue. Everyone living their lives in those tiny houses so far away, unaware of the struggle happening in the house tucked within the trees in the middle of cornfields.

Deadlocked, one of them would weaken eventually. Not waiting to discover which, Abbie knew she had to do something. That damned syringe still pointing down at her.

Kaleigh's face thrust forward—glowing purple eyes—filling Mrs. Thummel's. "*K-k-k-kill* her, mommy!" the little girl said.

Startled, Abbie's insides, perhaps her soul, leaped back within herself when her body could not. Her locked arms never buckled, somehow extending their reach another inch or so to keep the thing away.

Equally bizarre, Abbie had forgotten all about Kaleigh, who hadn't emerged for some time until now. What had started as mano-a-mano (hand-to-hand) and woman-to-woman never was. Not even physically. No, this fight had been two-on-one all along.

Under those purple eyes appeared a teeth-grinding smile—Mrs. Thummel's. Teeth separated as her mouth opened and a violent war cry escaped, powered by her daughter's expressed wishes: *'K-k-k-kill her, mommy!'*

"Yesyesyes!" mother agreed as her downforce on Abbie weighed heavy on the girl's shaking arms, erasing that inch and then some that Abbie had gained.

Frantically, Abbie wiggled her body like a snake, scooching away from Mrs. Thummel toward the far side of the bed against the wall as far as she could with her ankles still roped to the bed. Pushing on Missus at an angle, she let go and pulled her arms back. Missus fell forward—and so did the needle.

It plunged through the loose fabric of Abbie's shirt, the bedding, and mattress until Abbie sat up to work on freeing her ankles, pulling the needle out of the bed, now dangling in her shirt.

Mrs. Thummel's head raised, hair covering the faces. Abbie wailed down on them with both fists, letting out her own war cry. Missus' head cowered in self-defense.

But not before noticing the needle dangling in the sitter's shirt. It could still be done. All it needed was a thrust forward. Her bony hand reached for the needle.

Abbie clubbed one arm on the woman while she worked on freeing an ankle.

Missus' head raised; purple eyes glowed out of a forest of crusted hair. *It's not safe to enter the woods.*

No, it wasn't. Abbie saw the needle and went for it.

Too late, Missus had it. Who pushed it toward the sitter in hopes it would stick.

The metal tip scraped Abbie's side. A bend of the torso had kept it from entering.

Wrapping both hands around Missus' holding the needle, Abbie pushed down toward the bed, tearing a gash in her shirt.

Bent over in an awkward position, Missus pulled her body back over her feet, but, with Abbie bracing her hand to the bed, she was still bent over.

One of Abbie's ankles felt entirely free from her leg, whipping about during the struggle. There was still rope around the other one, still too tight to break free, but loose enough to rotate an ankle in. So, Abbie transitioned from her butt onto a knee. A hand let go of Missus' and reached back to work on that stubborn cord.

With both in awkward postures, it was difficult for either one to gain an advantage in fighting for the needle.

A key untying loosened the rope around Abbie's ankle enough to pull her foot through.

A slap sounded when Missus' freehand smacked the back of Abbie's hands.

Then, a smack from Abbie's untying hand joining the *druggy* party at the needle. They fought for it, manos-a-manos.

Feeling the wall at her feet, Abbie turned her body and pushed against it.

Lips covered teeth as the gritty smile on Missus' face transformed into surprised effort. Sacrificial love for her kids overwhelmed her. The blue of Kaleigh's eyes surfaced and retreated behind the red of her mother's. Mrs. Thummel violently threw her head forward, head-butting Abbie.

A crack sounded when the cranium rammed into the bridge of Abbie's nose. Pain zeroed in there and Abbie's eyes watered, still seeing the red eyes glow. Warm blood gathered quickly in her nostrils and ran down her lip. It tasted metallic.

Dazed, she prayed not to lose consciousness. Through blurred vision, an unbelievable observance, only seen in part but enough, made Abbie take a chance. For behind the haze, Mrs. Thummel swayed unsteadily with a hand on her forehead.

Seizing her opportunity, Abbie held both hands tight around Missus' on the needle and pushed her feet as hard as she could against the wall behind her, thrusting herself toward her attacker. Blood splattered out of her nose like paint from a swung brush.

Missus stumbled backward. The bed moved out from the wall where it had been since replacing Kaleigh's crib. The disturbance to the room bothered Missus, for Abbie could see it on her face.

Both refused to relinquish the needle.

Abbie's feet left the wall and gained traction on the bed. The momentum carried Mrs. Thummel's butt to the floor in a slow, controlled sit, while Abbie's feet churned on the top covers, slipping now and again.

With their arms stretched out, Abbie's hands still wrapped around Missus' around the needle, it looked as if Abbie laid on top of a cliff, reaching down for someone who had fallen over its edge.

The bedsheet wrinkled under Abbie's sneakers but held. The bed, however, did not. One side of the frame separated from the head and footboard legs and dropped on the shins of Missus. Snaps sounded. Headfirst, Abbie slid down the bed onto a screaming Mrs. Thummel, sending the woman flat on her back on the floor. Another snap sounded.

Heated pain spread through Mrs. Thummel's legs. Strangely, a similar warmth in her wrist intensified; the wrist of the hand that had held so tightly onto the needle.

Phobic with an extreme aversion to the murderous hybrid under her, Abbie pounded on the trees of the black forest, hoping tree trunks would protrude into those purple eyes. And only that phobia could be categorized as rational; everything else wasn't. Including Abbie. Who clubbed as hard as she could at those trees to reach the monster.

An onslaught of repeated blows clobbered the two faces until Kaleigh's went away and Missus' had darkened with blood.

At first, Abbie's fists felt numb, more like bricks than flesh and bone in her quest to survive. But as the beatdown went on, pain and swelling proved breaks and dislocations. She was hurting herself—the same as Missus' had done with the headbutt. Still, better that than death.

A defiant but debilitated Mrs. Thummel laid there, feeling herself slipping away. Pain from the metal bedframe digging into her shins as Abbie moved became pressure. Her pinned legs felt heavy, waterlogged. Only not with water, but blood. Blood-logged. When excruciating pain diminished as it had, it couldn't be good. And it wasn't.

A memory of Kayne and Kaleigh being placed in her arms after birth brought with it a flood of emotion. Hail, Satan, it was if she laid in the hospital bed now, feeling about how she had that day—beaten up and exhausted. Pregnancies burden a woman's body in ways not fully understood by men. It was so real, she could feel them in each arm. Two precious gifts that, at the time, she wanted to return. Full of regret and shame, she wished she had been a better mother when they were alive, knowing she was a better mother in their death. The fact that they hadn't died and were cryonicized prematurely wouldn't have changed that if she knew.

Other memories played in her mind. Of her

childhood. Dates. Her first time having sex. Meeting Hugh. Dates with Hugh. Her first time having sex with him. Getting married. The birth of their children. Married life. Parent life. The Halloween party. The accident. The death of her children. The basement. The agreement. And everything in between and since. Mrs. Thummel's life was flashing before her mind's eye. Of all the gods and deities and otherwise that she and Hugh had tried over the years, only one, Satan, the one who had brought her children back in the most unusual way, crossed her mind. The image wasn't pretty. Nor did it bring peace. At this point, whether it was accurate or conjured up in her mind, it didn't matter. For she would be moving on—she believed it. All these years, she believed in an afterlife, *'Satan rewards his living followers and punishes them in death.'*

Lying on Kaleigh's bedroom floor, she also believed she had been punished right along in this life and more punishment awaited her in death. A deal is a deal, so whatever may come.

Inside Mrs. Thummel, Kaleigh knew her mother was dying. Not from experience, because she hadn't died the night of the accident, but because the foreign finality of her mother's last moments made it known.

Kaleigh's face reappeared in her mother's and the six-year-old voice cried out through her mother's lips, "Mommy! Mommy! I want to stay with you!"

Startled, Abbie pounded on both faces, feeling threatened and adrenalized, keeping her in survival mode until she survived. The body under her softened, its breathing slowed, the face blackened; Kaleigh's face no longer there. All of it repulsed her enough to stop.

Exhausted, Abbie rolled off the body with throbbing, swelled, blood-filled, bloodstained hands.

For the first time, she saw the bedframe embedded in the woman's legs. Surreal, it looked fake, an optical illusion, tricking the eyes hours after trick-or-treat.

Lying on the floor beside the woman, Abbie tore her eyes away from the gruesome image only to see another. For layered within Missus' bludgeoned face was the young girl's face. Exactly when it had reappeared, she didn't know.

The moans coming out of the adult mouth on a blood-blackened, aged face did not, nor ever would, make sense. Utterances of the dead from the underworld weren't for the living, except when the living were dying, nearing death. Those final moments when understanding was understood, but too late to heed the advice the dead shouted from under the living's feet or down from overhead.

Abbie clubbed her again. It just happened. Nothing conscious about it.

Kaleigh scowled.

Mrs. Thummel laid motionless on the floor; her dress curled up to her thighs, one leg straight, the other slightly bent, but both pinched under the collapsed bed. A long arm curved above her head, the other tucked awkwardly under her body. Just below her pendant, the needle stuck out of the center of her chest, as her black dress concealed the blood around it. Head tilted, face sagging with pores weighed down by blood, she looked at Abbie with those red eyes, not glowing as brightly as they had before.

Kaleigh's presence comforted Nora that she would not die alone; a presence closer than Hugh or anyone else could ever be.

As the red light in Nora's eyes faded, more blue shined through—Kaleigh's, the mother comforted her child, "I know, sweet child. My baby. Mommy's here."

A better mother in death.

A forceful blow from the heel of Abbie's sneaker to Missus' forehead ended the thought.

"Shutupshutupshutup!" Abbie yelled. The girl had spun on the floor like a breakdancer to get into a good kicking position.

"Don't go, Mommy! Please don't go! I want to stay with you!"

Abbie heel-kicked the conversing head.

"I'm sorry…"

Over and over again, when it wouldn't shut up.

"… dear. So … sorry. I wish … I … was … a … bet…"

"NO, MOMMY! NO! HOW AM I GOING TO LIVE WITHOUT YOU?"

A question asked all the time, but never more relevant than this particular situation as Kaleigh witnessed her mother's spirit leave her body.

Madness ensued. Both worlds, physical and spiritual, coexisted in Kaleigh's bedroom on the second floor of this secluded house surrounded by cornfields. Fatigued and lying on the floor beside Mrs. Thummel's still body, Abbie stared, ignorant of the spirit rising out of it like the smoke of a blown-out candle. Relaxed lips that will never move again without its operator silenced the daughter. As far as Abbie knew, not hearing another word.

Physical and spiritual realms had also coexisted in the being once known as Mrs. Nora Thummel. Who, like anyone who had ever lived, had loved ones and friends who said *goodbye*, as the six-year-old daughter had, *and* those, like Abbie, who expressed *good riddance.*

Madness had always existed in this house. It wasn't

just tonight. There had been many nights when Halloween ended and Allhallows began where the physical and spiritual comingled through a portal in the basement.

Don't be alarmed. This cohabiting had always existed in every person who had ever lived. Look no farther than the reflection in the mirror. For that person looking back acts as a portal of sorts, a carrier transporting a spirit into the physical world—body and spirit born into the world together.

Funny how the body wasn't needed at departure. Nora's spirit abandoned it. So, ignoring the soul or any other layers that make up a person, let's agree two parts are confusing enough. It begs the question: Who was Nora, really? Was she a good-spirited woman with an evil-willed flesh? If so, why had the flesh won? Was it because the body was physical? Were both evil? Why does only a portion of a person move on?—assuming a portion does—as Nora's spirit rose out of her body.

Kaleigh saw it—Abbie didn't. And she was lying on the floor beside the body. Both have spirits to see it but existed in different circumstances.

Who gives a shit? The broad had killed or played a part in killing—*what?*—somewhere between thirty to sixty children or so over the years, many in more gruesome manners than administering a lethal injection. Which, Abbie had escaped.

Sweat adhered Abbie's shirt to her body. Her face felt gross and sticky, gelled with blood. Throbs in her bloodied nose and bloodstained, swelled hands exacerbated the pain. Each one pulsated to their own beat, alternating, ensuring the girl received a continuous dosage of pain.

Mrs. Thummel felt nothing, of course, not anymore,

not after the lethal injection. Including, Kaleigh's panicked entity inside her dead body, trying to align things to animate it.

Abbie had since gotten herself up off the floor. Wiping her hands on her shirt, she winced and had to stop because it hurt like hell. Her hands were about as sensitive as two puss-filled zits. Contact with anything triggered pain.

No matter. A little pain in exchange for her life seemed fair. A last look at her triumph—

Mrs. Thummel's eyes glowed.

Abbie's eyes widened with fear. It's not just the eyes glowing; it's blue eyes moving behind inanimate, pale-red ones—dark purple where they converge.

Instinctively, Abbie's right foot smashed down onto Missus' drooping face. Both blue circles of Kaleigh's eyes dimmed and shrank as she retreated deeper inside her mother's corpse.

Abbie raised her foot again, knee cocked, ready to stomp.

Nothing more happened, so Abbie lowered her foot.

A wind brushed up against the side of Abbie, popping goosebumps all over her body. A long, drawn-out *Mooooom-my!* faintly sounded within the wind.

It could have been Abbie hearing things, for the wind had made many a believer before, but she knew it was Kaleigh.

And it was Kaleigh, forced out of her mother's body, swooshing across her bedroom, through the opening behind the bookshelf, into the silver canister, and slamming into her own frozen body.

Kaleigh cried out, "Mommy! Mommy! Where are you, Mommy? We didn't get a soul, Mommy!" Her wailing echoed inside her altered body as if vacant.

"Mommy! Mommy! Why didn't I go to heaven, Mommy? Why did I stay here?"

Abbie no longer heard Kaleigh. Without Nora, a portal in her own right, different realms of existence made sure of that.

Paralyzed by the brush with half-death, she still felt it, although she no longer felt the wind. Survival instincts kicked in and the same old song sung and played one too many times for one show—for one night—goaded once more: *I need to run!*

Before she knew it, she was out of the bedroom and knee-pumping down the littered stairs.

30

Mr. Thummel and Kayne were just about finished getting everything set-up in the basement, when Kayne yelled inside his father, "NO, MOMMY! NO!"

"Geez, son! What it is?"

"Daddy! Daddy! It's Mommy!"

"Well, what?" Mister said, coming off like any impatient father.

"She's *dead*, Daddy!"

Taken back by his son's words, the father stopped what he was doing and said, "It's part of it, son. It has to be done."

"No! *Mommy! Mommy's dead!*"

The conversation had occurred out of the same mouth—Mister's—as if two personalities chitchatted out of someone suffering from multiple personality disorder.

The father dropped what was in his hands and ran up the basement stairs in his pinstriped suit, striding two steps at a time in black dress shoes.

As the Gomez-goof ascended, Abbie came running down the hallway. For a brief moment, back at the foyer, she had contemplated trying the front door to see if it would open—or lock itself as it had before. That scared her the most. Seeing that again would cost too much. Physically, mentally, emotionally, spiritually, there wasn't much left in each tank and would probably cost her her life. Besides, why waste time and effort messing with the front door only to have to go around the house to get to the back. So down the hall and past the basement door, she ran. For this time, the girl knew where she was going. She had a train to catch. An all-out sprint to the station was her only chance.

Into the kitchen and out the back door, Abbie went when Mr. Thummel emerged out of the basement into the hallway, the chain of his pocket watch swinging against the pocket of his double-breasted suit coat.

Chugging at a good clip across cornfields galore scared Abbie because she wasn't much of a runner. Looking at her, anyone would think she might be, but she wasn't. Short distances, she could hold her own. Across muddy cornfields in the dark after the night she had, not so much.

Lightning flashed as Abbie ran away from the house. Adrenaline from her spat with the ladies of the house still coursed through her veins; she tried to keep up. Revenge of reporting Mister fueled her, guessing Kayne would do time inside his father.

Mister clomped a couple of hard steps toward the front of the house to go upstairs to check on Nora until he heard the wind whisper through the kitchen.

When he backtracked and swung the basement door closed to check the kitchen, the back door was open, leaves rolling his direction across the linoleum floor. As he thought, his eyes glanced up toward the second floor; then he turned and ran toward the back door after Abbie.

Raindrops bulleted toward the Earth so fast and hard they bounced off the ground. Standing in the doorway, Mister had to locate her; otherwise, he would be expending energy in a chase and not chasing anything. No longer a spring chicken, he couldn't do that, especially after running her down earlier.

Through the rain and darkness, a flash of color at the edge of the yard caught his attention and then went away. Lightning flickered on and off like a strobe light, and, *yes*, it was Abbie, running away from the house toward the cornfield. Beyond her and the field were the tiny lights and faint outline of the train station.

For a few seconds, one flash remained on her like a spotlight; then everything went dark. Another flash of light brightened the back of the house when Mister took off after her.

His dress shoes sloshed in the waterlogged ground. They weren't ideal for this kind of shit, running, and killing, and whatnot, yet black dress shoes were part of the gig year-after-year.

Black sneakers next year, he thought. *A more casual, progressive Gomez to bring him up to speed with the times. Hail, Satan!*

And people think only weird thoughts come to those in peril or about to die. *Wrong!* Killers think stranger shit than most. Like trees have hair and bark *woof! woof!*, leaves grow on dogs, and green beer comes out their sex organs and nipples. Backasswards, right?

But they're killers for Satan's sake. And probably not far from the truth.

Kayne yelled through his father to Abbie, "*Hey! Hey! Why you want to play tag? … Okay. We can play tag. I'll be it first.*"

Only a whistle of the train, pulling into the station, yelled back, informing Mister it was damned near six a.m. Hallowmas.

Mud caked Abbie's sneakers. Every time they came up out of the cornfield, they pulled up more. And every time they sank into the ground, the more likely they would stay there. Everything else tonight had betrayed her, so why not the field. Even the fact that they were harvested said something. Some cornstalks for cover would be helpful right now.

Then there was the rain. It had to be the hardest rain Abbie had ever witnessed in her young life. Every drop, exploding on her head, hurt like the devil spit them. Wrong direction, of course, but maybe he was visiting with God as he had done in times past. The Almighty must be offering Abbie to him right now, as he had done to poor Job.

And cold that rain was on her drenched head and body. Not arctic cold, but when the wind howled, it was damned close.

Mr. Thummel's night hadn't gone any better. Easily the worst he could remember. And if Nora—

His drenched suit weighed him down. Numerous times he had nearly lost a shoe. A sucking sound occurred every time he pulled a foot out of the mud. Oh, to be a kid again. His six-year-old son giggled because, to him, they sounded like farts. *Giggling Giggins!*

The father's running made the boy feel free, like an eagle soaring toward its prey.

This playful youthfulness and wondering about Nora fueled Hugh through the elements—for a second time tonight.

Abbie sneaked a peek over her shoulder. The metal chain, dangling from Mr. Thummel's breast pocket, winked at her.

OH, GOD! NO! PLE…

A second whistle drowned out her thought. The station still so far away.

Inside his father and in spirit, Kayne chased after her, yelling out in a young boy's voice, "Kill her, Daddy! She killed Mommy!"

There it was again, Hugh thought. *He said it again. Oh, Nora, my Bea, don't be—*

"Kill her, Daddy! For Mommy! Mommy, Daddy!"

With the cadence, Mister gained ground. Together, he and his son pursued with that intent. Not only for the kids' sake but vengefully if indeed Nora was dead.

A soul for a soul to take
The souls in terrible danger
One soul will do if at least twice their age
But the unfortunate soul gets double their rage

Kayne helped to spirit on his father's body into a faster gear. They were catching up to *the unfortunate soul*, Abbie, with *double their rage*, Nora's son and husband, who also thought of Kaleigh, then pushed her out of his mind.

Abbie's heavy breathing and the rain, splatting against her wet head and clothes, sounded magnified. So did the train's whistle, carrying over the field, slicing through the wind, and dodging the rain. The lights over there so far away.

The whistle stopped.

The usual sounds of the chase returned. Everything

raw. As raw as in the bedroom with Mrs. Thummel.

Abbie turned her head a fraction and faced forward again.

Close now, Mr. Thummel reached out for her, just missing.

In cadence, they both sloshed through the mud, maintaining less than a two-foot interval between them.

The gap closed; he reached for her again.

"No!" the unfortunate soul released, feeling fingertips brush her back.

The touch kicked Abbie into a faster gear. Her legs felt out of control, running so fast. Adrenalized. Supercharged. Divine intervention. She chose life, perhaps, fate had, too. Life was simple. She needed to run! Someone or something had told her that all night. Some live to run. Try running to live. How long this power would last, how long she would last at this pace, she didn't know. Didn't want to know.

Raindrops slapped the mud. So did the leather bottoms of Mister's shoes as he ran, sounding more distant now. His breathing not as close.

Abbie snuck a peek over her shoulder. The gap had widened between them, but he was still coming.

I choose me! Choose me, fate!

A solid thud against the toe of her left sneaker threw what running form and rhythm she had out of whack. A sudden, jarring shock vibrated up her left leg, spreading a tingling sensation throughout her body from hitting something solid on the ground.

Sticking out of the ground, a severed cornstalk from harvest had impeded her progress, abruptly slowing her momentum. Bent over with her torso parallel with the ground, Abbie fought to stay on her feet. Rain stung her back through her shirt. Hanging, drenched hair made it more difficult to see than it already was.

In slow, elongated steps, her legs stretched under her body like a trotting ostrich, searching for balance. One leg forward, then the other, alternating until her back foot slid out from underneath her before she could get her front foot down. Forward momentum had her falling face-first with her arms out like a baseball player coming in for a slide to steal a base.

In an aisle between chopped-off cornstalks, she landed in the mud, sliding on her belly. Her feet raised off the ground and teetered her face into the cakey dirt, breaking her to a stop. Her cell phone slid out of her back pocket, surfed over the back of her body, and stuck in the mud near her head.

Heavy breathing came up from behind. Suction sounds, slow and deliberate, moved along the sitter's body toward her head. A squish to her left, then a black shoe and clinging pant leg appeared in her view to the right.

Mr. Thummel stood over her, hair matted to his head, pale skin, the drenched double-breasted pinstriped suit hanging on his thin frame. When he opened his mouth, Kayne spoke for his out-of-breath father, "I caught you!"

When Abbie tried getting up, her hands disappeared in the mud. Her chest barely off the ground, a foot to her back pressed her back down.

Abbie laid there, the front of her body and the side of her head in cold, wet mud. Contradictions, part of her full of emotion, another part unfeeling, kept her in neutral. Right up to the end, if this was the end, it felt like the end, life confused her—as it does everybody. A sixteen-year-old shouldn't understand, most would say. If life couldn't possibly be understood in that amount of time, then when does understanding come? Does it?

Neutral. Indifferent. Not caring one way or the other. Maybe that was understanding. If so, in the end, it had come.

Without much fight left, what could she do? Fighting fate, God, herself, others, and life, in general, had expended, expended, expended, and they had all took, took, took and never gave anything back.

Abbie sat her chin in the mud. Nothing around but cornfields galore. The damn train station so far away. Another warning whistle sounded. Lights on the train reminded her of lightning bugs, a swarm of them flying in line toward the station.

Something oppressive with force dropped on her back, forcing air out of her. Totally unexpected and will-breaking.

Mister had decided to plop down and take a seat. He turned his pale face toward the sky and drank rain, smiling, and laughing, tonguing his lips.

His hips began to move in a circular motion in rhythm with his tongue tracing his lips. Rain splashed his face. He looked down at the teen under him, rubbing his butt on the small of her back.

"Whatta doin, Daddy?" Kayne asked his father.

A look of confused shame replaced the pleasure on Mister's face—the same as in the kitchen when he had stroked Abbie's beautiful auburn hair.

He stood and barked, "Roll over!"

Sorely, Abbie rolled over onto her back. A severed cornstalk poked into her shoulder blade. As if it had prodded her, she started to sit up. A muddy dress shoe met her face, causing her nose to bleed again and sending her down onto that protruding cornstalk. The blow, along with Mrs. Thummel's head-butt earlier, were enough to concuss her.

Mister plopped his butt on her stomach, knocking more wind out of her. The cornstalk poked through her shirt and into her shoulder blade, breaking skin before crunching under the weight, while Mister scooched his ass around on her stomach as if to remove any remaining air. Only someone as sick as he could appreciate his expert methodology in handling such affairs. Affairs thoroughly enjoyed this time of year.

"You killed my Mommy!" Kayne said.

"And you killed my wife!" Mister grunted while cuffing his hands over her wrists and pinning her arms in the mud.

Assuming her left hand was her weakest, he let go of it and turned his head to the left to protect his face as he untied his black tie.

Abbie's left arm flailed, landing only glancing blows.

Through fogged vision, Abbie saw Mister looking down at her. Hair matted to his head as if over-greased. A face as pale as the moon when the sun reflects off it. Behind it, a dark purple sky scratched with vertical lines of crystal clear raindrops falling. There were so many that they resembled tinsel streaming from the sky. And tonguing his lips, he was. Tonguing thin, glistening lips—and enjoying it. Blue eyes wandered under brown. Deforming shadows of another nose and mouth on the same face, yet two faces comingling like absorbed twins.

Instead of Mr. Thummel's eyes glowing like his wife's had, his dung-browns suddenly blackened and hardened into glossy marbles, while Kayne's glowed behind them—not blue—now a pale yellow, the color of Venus as seen from Earth—Kayne, the son of the morning star. For Kayne and Kaleigh had two fathers because of the sins of the father, Hugh: drinking and driving with two small children in the vehicle and cryonizing his children when they weren't dead.

Inexplicably, father's voice mixed with his son's, as they both spoke, "You're (Na—) going (now) to (I'm) die (going) you (to) fucking (kill) bitch! (you!)"

For the umpteenth time, it was almost impossible for Abbie to comprehend what she saw and heard, as she looked up at them and them down at her.

The rain paused. Other than a few straggling drops slapping on and around them, the scratches that had lined the sky were now filled in. The timing of the stoppage was nothing less than eerie. It was as if the Earth waited to see what would happen next. Steam fogged over the surface of the ground.

Staring at the monster over her, Abbie wondered why the voice from earlier wasn't telling her she needed to run. Or do anything else for that matter. Perhaps, it, too, had become neutral. Or it knew something she didn't.

As quickly as it had stopped, the sky opened again into a downpour, pelting them and the muddy ground with large drops.

So did Abbie's floodgates. Her tears mixed with Earth's rain. It just came, her having no control over it. Emotion spewed out of the sixteen-year-old girl into the world. Pain mostly. Lots and lots of pain. And the more she fought it, the easier it flowed, for she didn't want to give it to him—her pain.

Brakes squealed as the train slowed to a stop at the station. The locomotive whistled long one final time.

Hurriedly and violently, Mister let Abbie's other arm go and laid flat against her, his weight driving her backside deeper into the mud. Fists swung wildly at his head as he wrapped the tie around the back of her neck.

The flurry didn't last long. Punched swings slowed as Mister worked—until they stopped. Partly, the will to fight in Abbie had taken flight, departed to somewhere she couldn't find and it would take too much effort to track down. It wasn't in the house, because she had brought it outside. It could be anywhere now.

Mostly, throwing punches hurt too damn much. Swollen hands, full of fractured and broken bones, were too sore and too fragile to change things. Tiny beanbags would never get this monster off her. A far cry from the bricks she had pummeled Missus with in Kaleigh's bedroom.

Tears streamed down her face, camouflaged by the rain, her tired, wincing eyes full of despair. She thought once more, *Do we choose our life's path, or does fate choose for us?*, and then, *I didn't choose this.* She had her answer.

Clenching both ends of his tie, the double-spirited, double-raged avenger sat up on the sitter's stomach and crisscrossed it over her Adam's apple, pulling as tightly as he could in opposite directions, using all of his leverage to crush her throat.

Gasping for air, Abbie threw those beanbag hands at his head and then tried sliding her fingers between the tie and her neck, but it was too tight for even the slimmest of fingers. Her legs kicked up, down, and around on the muddy cornfield, flailing, splashing mud and water. Attempts at kneeing him in the back failed, the angle all wrong.

Kayne urged on his daddy, "Kill her, Daddy! She killed Mommy!"

In a quest to end her, Mr. Thummel licked his bottom lip, the rest of his face contorted in effort, now blending in with early morning's darkness, his arms shaking from pulling the tie.

Abbie's flailing legs slowed down, her purplish face camouflaged in the mud, as dawn worked on breaking through.

I'm sorry, Mom.

At death's door, Abbie's short life zoomed across her mind's eye, fast-forwarding through one long video, inexplicitly having time to see every significant moment only another could have captured as if someone had recorded her life as she lived it. Even seeing now, this very moment as if watching live TV: Mr. Thummel on his knees in the cornfield—that's how it looked because she wasn't visible so far down in the mud—and choking her as rain scratched the sky.

How? Who?

Whether there was another world beyond this one or not, leaving this one was significant.

Shortly after the 6 a.m. train had entered the station behind schedule, Mr. Thummel stood over her body, victorious, wanting to yell like an Indian after a scalping, but knew not to. Inside, Kayne does it for him, his little six-year-old voice sounded cute to his father rather than frightening, but the emotion behind it stirred him just the same. Although he hadn't seen it for himself, he now knew he had lost his wife, the boy his mother. For his son had said so, but his son's war cry had confirmed it.

Mister reached down, picked Abbie's cell phone out of the mud, and slid it in the inside pocket of his suit jacket. It will be destroyed like all the others.

In the pouring rain, Mr. Thummel carried Abbie's

body in a fireman's carry—his tie still dangling around her neck—trudging through the cornfield, across the yard, and disappearing into the well of the concrete steps leading to the basement, descending like a dark angel taking her to hell.

31

The all-nighter had caught up with everyone working and waiting at the state police station in Station Flat. Stale coffee left on burners too long, uneaten fast food on desks for hours, residual smoke on the clothes of smokers, body odor, and halitosis polluted the air inside. Quiet as any night should be; uncomfortably foul as it should be under the circumstances. Officers and civvies not on the job rested, even closed their eyes, but never nodded off. Time was always of the essence in missing person cases and tonight ticked by without a break.

Blip!...Blip!...Blip! "*Hey. Hey,* everyone. We have a signal," the investigating officer said, punching keys on a keyboard as others on the search team gathered around.

"*Juuust* a bit longer." His fingers tapped keys faster.

"*Aaaaaand*—Yes!" Half-turning his head while keeping his eyes on the screen, he read aloud, "6 Balmar Road, Station Knoll."

Scrambling, everyone disbursed to their positions.

"All units. All units. We have a 207 at 6 Balmar Road, Station Knoll. All units. All units. We have a 207 at 6 Balmar Road, Station Knoll."

Abbie's cell phone had landed in the mud just outside the dead zone long enough for the police to pick up a signal.

32

In gloomy-gray dawn, a convoy of three police cars traveled along a dirt road, flanked on both sides by cleared cornfields. Rain pummeled their windshields, the wipers unable to keep up. The navigation system in the lead car informed the officers they were on Balmar Road and will reach their destination of 6 Balmar Road in Station Knoll in eight hundred feet. The dirt road became a paved surface.

The passenger officer looked around and said, "There's nothing but cornfields out here. The nav must be batty."

The driver peeked over at his partner, then returned to the road. His hand regripped the steering wheel as he wondered the same thing.

Up ahead, tucked among a group of trees, straight edges of a structure became visible.

"I'll be damned," the passenger said, staring.

After a paralyzed lapse, he reported in to the station that they were approaching their target location.

The driver turned off the headlights and the other two cruisers followed suit. The navigation system announced they had reached their destination, as the motorcade rolled quietly from the clearing into the grove.

From their approach, there were no vehicles in view. A light shined out of the open back door; otherwise, the rest of the house appeared dark, as did the barn on the left.

Behind the house, all three squad cars parked in a spread-triangular formation. Raindrops plopped on metal roofs and glass windshields as the officers discussed strategy and assignments over the radio. After testing their earpieces, shoulder mics, and checking their weapons, the teams were ready to move.

Tactically, with weapons drawn, they exited their vehicles. Rain pelted the top of their flat covers like a drum. Team three headed for the barn. Team two approached the house to sweep its perimeter. Team one approached the house toward the open door.

Weapons raised to the ready, team one negotiated the back door with experience and training, entering the kitchen. A pile of wet leaves, just inside the door, trailed to dryer ones sprawled all over the linoleum floor. No doubt, the door had been open for some time. Center kitchen, a chair faced the back door. Rope among the leaves by the chair's front legs and more near the back were signs something wicked had happened here.

An officer from team three noticed a Chrysler Fifth Avenue parked behind the barn, matching the *'all-black'* description given by Abbie's mom and called it into the station. Teams one and two heard the call.

Inside the house, the officers closed the back door, cleared the kitchen, and moved into the hallway.

From the basement, Mr. Thummel heard a creak in the floor above his head and looked up. Not hearing anything more, he assumed it was the house creaking from the wind and went back to work.

In the hall, a mirror hung off-kilter on the wall. Under a rectangular accent table, flush against the wall of the stairs, laid a small lamp on its side. Not far from it, ceramic pieces of a knick-knack; its crumbs still sprinkled in the middle of the hall floor.

To Sergeant Haskins, it seemed someone had merely kicked them under the table to get them out from the middle of the walkway. He looked at his partner and they both knew that something had happened here.

Slowly and quietly, Haskins opened the basement door a crack, while his partner pointed his pistol at the ready. Lights were on below. Hearing noises, Haskins cautiously closed the door.

It squeaked.

Mister stopped what he was doing and listened. Cautiously, he walked over to the bottom of the steps and peeked up.

Upstairs, in the hallway, Haskins showed his teeth, just waiting for the steps to creak from whoever was in the basement to investigate the sound. His partner double-clutched the pistol's grip.

The door closed, no one there, and no more sounds, Mr. Thummel returned to his task.

Not hearing anything, Haskins nodded to his partner to keep an eye on the door and retreated to the kitchen. Knowing the other teams were listening, with few words and nothing more than a whisper, he called into the station and reported that there was at least one person in the basement, but without a visual, he couldn't say for sure how many or their identities.

The officers of team two came upon the well leading to the basement. Light shined out the broken door, reflecting on wet concrete steps. Stealthily, one officer maneuvered down the steps, avoiding broken glass, while the other officer stood at the ready at the top of the steps, pointing his weapon down the stairs.

Halfway down, the lead officer stopped and crouched, able to see through the shattered door into the basement. He removed his cover, lying it upside-down on a step behind him, and motioned for the other officer to do the same because the rain pelting it made too much noise and they couldn't afford to have them give away their location.

The crouched officer called into the station, mostly for the benefit of teams one and three, whispering, "Copy. Basement verified. We have a visual. Male. Unknown. Wearing a white lab coat. Appears to be alone, but can't verify. Copy."

In the hallway, Sergeant Haskins replied, "Copy that. There's only one way to verify. Copy."

The officer, crouching on the steps, agreed. "Copy. On your *go*. Copy."

"Copy that. On my *go*."

At the station, those listening on the radio empathized with the officers as if they were the ones at the scene.

Despite the activity at the house, team three continued their search of the barn.

In the hallway, with the basement door cracked, Haskins nodded to his partner, then whispered over the mic, *"Go."*

On the concrete steps outside, the crouched officer nodded to his partner.

Both teams converged on the basement; team one down the basement stairs inside the house; team two down the concrete steps outside.

"Police officers!" the lead officer of team two said, getting there first. "Hands up!"

Both officers pointed their pistols at the guy in the lab coat. They focused on him, but their eyes wandered because there was a lot to take in. Ruts in the floor circled around near their feet. A bunch of grooves spread from where they stood. Black candles, lit and evenly spaced, seemed particularly positioned. To their right, a metal folding chair, having black material draped over its backrest and things on the seat. A washer and dryer. Metal barrels—a bunch of them. Two large cardboard boxes.

Having farther to go, Sergeant Haskins and his partner reached the bottom of the steps and flanked the man in the white lab coat, pointing their pistols at him.

Near the center of the hexagram, Mr. Thummel stood beside a contraption and continued to work as if the officers weren't there.

Overloaded by what they were seeing, it took Haskins and his partner a moment to process their surroundings. The unusualness of it made it more difficult for all of the officers, but they quickly adapted.

Knowing his guys had a bead on this creampuff, Haskins took the liberty of gawking longer than the rest. When his eyes retreated back to his feet, they wandered over to the basement steps. What he saw there brought this whole mess to a head.

A disorienting haze clouded his vision as he looked up from what he saw, turned across the room with a man in white and two officers behind, and, finally, seeing his partner on his left. Making a clicking sound with his mouth, Haskins got the attention of his partner. A slight nod of the head, along with a shift of the eyes, told his partner where to look.

On the dirt by the base of the stairs laid a cell phone on a balled-up pile of muddied clothes on top of muddy sneakers—everything that would belong to a typical teenaged girl.

Sergeant Haskins steadied himself and his pistol, seeing his partner's facial expression.

"Abbie!" Haskins said, looking around the room. "My name is Officer Haskins. If you're in the basement, I need you to come out from where you are—*slowly*."

Inside the barn, team three relayed information with the station and units one and two in the basement.

"Copy. Visual of an *all-black* car parked behind the barn with verified registration to a Eugene and Beatrice Giggins, *not* Hugh and Nora Thummel. Repeat. Vehicle registered to a Eugene and Beatrice Giggins, NOT Hugh and Nora Thummel. Copy."

33

In the basement, Sergeant Haskins shot one of those *What the hell is going on here?* looks at his partner, then replied, "Copy that."

Scouring the basement, Haskins didn't see any movement—no sign of Abbie.

"I said, hands in the air," the lead from team two said. "Now!"

Ignoring the officer, Mr. Thummel worked, monitoring a mechanical apparatus with pumps and hoses attached to a side of what looked like a feeding trough. Metal poles framed it out with silver tarp on all sides. No sag suggested the bottom must be solid rather than a tarp. Wide enough and long enough for a person—

Damnitdamnitdamnit! Haskins hated when his mind thought the worst. Most of the time, that was his job.

He hated more being right. That contraption looked like a gurney from a hospital. None like any he had ever seen. Not tarped like this one. But a gurney nonetheless.

His partner and the other officers probably noticed it, too, but what good would it do stating the obvious. Nothing, that's what. They had a job to do.

Haskins went from *thinking* the worst to *fearing* the worst. A gargantuan difference. When a thought became a feeling, it usually meant he was right. Confirmed. Not a hundred percent, of course, but damn near.

Composure. He had to maintain his composure. His team appeared composed, but one never knew what buzzed around inside another officer, especially with their finger on a trigger.

And no one knew this better than Haskins. Assholes, like this lab-coat-wearing sphincter, were never wiped and always stunk. Sometimes the only way to get rid of the smell for good was by wiping them out completely. Even cops scratch at this itch and carrying a gun didn't help. It's a wonder there weren't more cop shootings. No one could tolerate everybody all the time. Yet, as a whole, cops do.

Sergeant Haskins suffered that itch right now—in his trigger finger—wanting to rub it against the trigger for some relief. Expressions on the other officers said they, too, suffered from the same ailment.

"Last time!" leader from two said. "Hands up! Right now, get 'em up."

Soon intolerance would lead to bloodlust for this guy. If this prick didn't cooperate pronto, the coroner was going to find four hundred rounds in his body. Probably more, because, nowadays, cops carried backup rounds on them, even around these parts.

"Has, his hands aren't up!" the lead officer from team two said to Haskins, not wanting to use his full name.

"I see," Sergeant Haskins said. "Control that itch."

In an athletic stance, head tilted behind a raised pistol, finger on the trigger, Haskins moved slowly toward the man, asking, "Are you, Hugh Thummel?"

The man, as pale as his white lab coat, continued to work.

Moving closer, Haskins asked, "Is your name, Eugene Giggins?"

Mr. Hugh Thummel, a. k. a. Eugene Giggins, stopped working and looked up from the tarped contraption.

Sergeant Haskins stopped, still aiming the pistol.

Slowly, Thummel turned his head and peeked over his shoulder at Sergeant Haskins.

"I want to smoke this guy…"

"Shut up!" Haskins commanded the other officer from team two.

Without turning his head, Thummel glanced at the blurting officer.

"You hear that," Haskins asked, moving closer. "We've all got the itch. If you don't get those hands in the air, you're going to find out how bad."

Close enough now for Haskins to see over the top pole and tarp of the *gurney*, it appeared to be filled with ice.

Thummel's eyes returned to Haskins as he turned to face him.

Squared up to Haskins was a tall, pale, lanky, jet-black-haired male, wearing what appeared to be a suit under an unbuttoned lab coat; the pinstriped slacks wet and muddied, as were his dress shoes. Strange, this fellow, a little off-kilter. Something—his face. Blurred. Scratched. Not as clear for some reason. Haskins stretched his eyes and blinked.

Nothing was wrong with Sergeant Haskins' eyes. Everything was wrong with Thummel's face. It appeared disfigured, jumbled—and it was. For the man in the lab coat wasn't looking with two eyes, but four; two sets of facial features coexisting on the same face.

Haskins straightened his head from behind his pistol.

The four eyes on the man's face held their stare, moving among each other like a distorted photograph. One pair brightened a pale-yellow; at their center, the other pair, black diamonds.

Black-eyed Susans, Haskins thought. Of all things, Black-eyed Susans.

A small boy's voice spoke out of Thummel's mouth, "Are they here because of mommy?"

"No," the father said in an adult voice. "They're here for us."

Surprisingly quick, Mr. Thummel, a.k.a. Mr. Giggins, bent down, reaching for something under the gurney.

The oddity of what had just occurred paralyzed Haskins and his partner into undefensive gawkiness. For they had seen it and heard it yet couldn't believe it. But no one more than Haskins, who had a front-row seat for the freakshow.

But this was no carnival. With weapons lowered and too shocked to think about anything else other than what they had witnessed, Haskins and his partner stood dumbfounded—and vulnerable.

Seeing something in Thummel's hand was enough to snap Sergeant Haskins out of his wonderment, running back and grabbing his partner's shoulder to get down.

"Team two, FIRE!" Haskins barked.

POP! POP!

Mr. Thummel's body contorted, arching back as if a ghost had kicked him two times mid-spine.

Police covers tumbled off Haskins and his partner as they fell willingly to the dirt floor.

Team two officers stood ready to fire again—wanting to—and did.

POP! POP!—POP!

Thummel's body jerked three times, his back arching farther each time.

The third shot came from the leader of team two, who scratched his itch a little longer, still pissed off this asshole hadn't raised his hands earlier.

Prone on the dirt, Haskins held a hand over his partner's head for him to stay down.

"Goddamnit, hold your fire!" Haskins snapped. "Hold your fire!"

An attitude of accomplishment filled team two as the leader stated indifferently, "All clear."

Haskins and his partner turned around to see Thummel, standing curved with his face toward the basement ceiling and an arm outstretched—holding a needle.

Sergeant Haskins and his partner snapped to their feet.

"Aw, damn, Sarge," his partner said, seeing the needle.

"Stay cool," Haskins said. "A weapon's still a weapon."

Mr. Thummel's body buckled sideways against the gurney. Ice rattled inside as if it were an ice chest.

Blood leaked out of his body and soaked through his clothes, darkening the lab coat at the bullet holes. Mister fell to his knees, nearly flipping the gurney over, but it ended up rolling and hitting the back of the basement stairs.

The non-lead officer from team two raised his pistol, fist around the grip, resting on an open hand for stability, and moved slowly toward the hunched-over body.

"Stay down!"

Mister fell forward, his face scraped dirt until he rolled over onto his side.

Waiting, every officer held their position.

When Thummel stopped moving, Haskins said to his partner, "Check him."

34

The officer moved toward the shot man on the ground, squatted next to him, and checked for a pulse.

Kayne felt his father slipping away. Like Kaleigh, it wasn't that he knew this from experience because he never died the night of the car crash. Unlike his sister, he wasn't quite sure how he knew—a sixth sense, perhaps.

Inside his father's container, the boy yelled, "NO, DADDY! *NOOOOO!*"

Vibration from the yell channeled through the officer's fingers acting as a conduit. Taken for a pulse, the officer said, "He's still ali... JESUS!—JESUS CHRIST!" His hand snapped back as he rose to his feet, startled, his face flushed. "Did you guys hear that?"

"Hear what?"

Confused, untrusting eyes of the pulse checker stared down at the man on the dirt floor, as he wiped his fingers on the front of his uniform.

"What did you hear?"

A gulp, then Haskins' partner answered, "A child's voice."

No one laughed. Standing around, they all stared at the body. For they all had heard a small boy's voice say earlier, *'Are they here because of mommy?'* but only Haskins and his partner had the unforgettable image of two faces coexisting on one face to go along with it.

"What did it say?"

Spiked hair sticking out of goosebumps on Haskins' partner tickled him—for they swayed, like wheat in the wind. Coming through him as it had, it was as if he had spoken the words himself.

'No, daddy, no,' he answered.

The words hovered there over Mister's body. In their own minds, each man heard the boy's voice speak, *'No, daddy, no.'* Amazing really, considering three officers had heard the boy's voice only once—Haskins' partner twice.

"Alright, break it up," Haskins said. "So, is there a pulse or not?"

"Yeah. Yeah, there was a pulse."

Was. Sergeant Haskins knew he couldn't get anybody to check for a pulse now. Once had been enough. He drew in air and released it.

"Alright. Let's request medical assistance," the Sergeant ordered.

The other three officers looked at each other, then at Sarge.

The officer, who had scratched his itch a little longer, resulting in an extra shot, couldn't believe it.

210

"What? Sarge—*come on!* I put two right between his blade and spine." He pointed to the blood spots in the lab coat for proof. "One or both must have hit his heart."

"You want to re-check my partner's work?" Haskins challenged. "Go ahead."

In contemplative hesitation by team two's leader, he shifted his weight from one leg to the other. His eyes lowered to the man at his feet, then up at the basement ceiling, then nowhere.

"All I'm saying, Sarge, is maybe we don't request assistance—if you catch my drift?"

There was no denying the proof. The proof was in the pudding—blood pudding. Two bloodstains near the heart and another below increased the chances that if this guy did have a pulse, he wouldn't for long. Maybe it and the guy were already gone.

"Goddamnit!" Haskins turned around and headed for what he took to be a *gurney* under the basement steps.

A sudden swoosh of air circulated out of Thummel's body as if it were a high-powered fan that had turned on. It didn't remain invisible for long. Dirt from the floor sucked into it and swirled around in a mini-tornado. Flames on the black candles flickered then blew out. The officers shielded their faces in the crooks of their arms. Mister's lab coat whipped like a white surrender flag in high winds. In a controlled manner, the funnel-shaped vortex tilted its angle from vertical to nearly horizontal. There was no evidence of who or what controlled it, or even how, but imagine a dirty drinking glass, sized for a giant, tipping over in slow motion onto its side without breaking.

Horizontally, the whirlwind moved toward the stairs. Baffling. Similar to a *black hole*, this cyclone had

211

sucked up dirt but nothing else, while simultaneously, emitting energy out from it, blowing things around, much like a *white hole*. So what was this reaching into an asshole, grabbing the dangling troublemaker, and pulling it back through the bunghole inside-out? Exactly. When things don't make sense, it's called the gray area. No different than gray water. Not pure enough to drink. Clean enough to use in non-digestive ways, such as toilet flushing. A step above black water which had been in contact with fecal matter. So what to call this then—a *gray hole*?

All right—the *gray hole* swept over the tarped-frame on wheels, shaking the ice in it like a rattle, and lifting it onto two wheels. If it weren't already up against the back of the steps, it surely would have tipped over.

The gray column curved, navigating around the staircase like a snake around a rock. At the bottom of the basement steps, the funnel angled itself with the stairs and launched up them as if a rocket were inside its own exhaust.

The white lab coat stilled. The two wheels on the gurney clanked when they returned to the dirt floor. One police cover was still visible; the other not. The black material had slid off the backrest of the chair; the cup and box of matches laid on the earthy floor beside the still upright chair. Two black candles had been knocked over. Some of the hexagram's design in the dirt had been erased. All the while, the house rumbled overhead.

By this time, team three had cleared the barn and had entered the house through the kitchen. One officer stood in the hallway while the other climbed the stairs to the second floor. Soaked to the bone, they were glad to get out of the rain.

The officer in the hallway started toward the front door when all of a sudden, as he walked, he felt his feet leave the floor, floating headfirst toward the ceiling. It was if Earth's gravity had ceased.

At first, it scared him, then, remaining upright, it was strangely fun.

Until, in a blur, the left side of his body slammed against the wall, stuck to it like a squashed bug, then crashed down on top of the accent table, destroying the only thing not damaged from earlier when this whole thing had begun.

Not long after, his partner, who had reported the vehicle behind the barn, was on his way up the stairs toward the bedrooms, stepping carefully among glass and debris, when a force from behind thrust him forward, sending him face-first into the steps. Lucky for him, his nose missed the corner, which might have killed him. Unlucky for him, his forehead and neck bore the brunt of a whiplashing collision with two edges of steps.

As he laid there prone on the stairs, cold air rolled right up his spine from the ass to the neck, shuffling his vertebra as it passed over. At first, the officer thought he might be suffering from paralysis; god forbid a paralyzing one. Then, no longer feeling the chilling sensation, the officer pushed-up off the step and stood. In doing so, his hands hurt. They were bloody. Speckles of glass stuck to them like salt on a couple of pretzels.

Something had re-stirred the debris on the steps. What, exactly, the officer couldn't say. Although he couldn't see it, he had felt it. And that was enough.

It has been a long time since he had been pushed like that. A very long time. Since grade-school. The last time he remembered feeling bullied and overmatched. An unforgettable experience that had cut so bad and deep he swore that when Billy the Bully had stabbed his pride, he left the whole damn hunting knife inside him—blade and handle. It was the last time anyone had messed with him, going on to become a star athlete in high school and, then, donning a police uniform. If anything, the *tip* of the blade, sticking out of his shoulder, had grown over into a *chip*.

But this wasn't Billy the Bully, although it had unexpectedly come from behind as Billy would have— the asshole.

Then, in looking at the top of the steps, he saw it. The tail end, perhaps. Of what, he didn't know. Not an asshole—a *gray hole*? A spinning vortex.

Whatever it was, it rounded the corner at the top of the steps, shaking the walls. Not long after, a loud bang occurred. To the officer on the steps, it sounded like a door had been slammed shut.

35

In the basement, the unnerved officer, who had checked Thummel's pulse, was not on board with rechecking it. Neither were the other officers. Being the Sergeant in charge, Haskins bent down and checked for a pulse. Looking up at the other officers, he shook his head there wasn't one.

Rather than questioning the pulse-checker on it, Haskins sought confirmation. Next in command, the leader from team two crouched, looked at the body, checked for a pulse, and agreed there wasn't one.

A collective relief took some of the edge off.

"Call it in," Haskins said, then blurted, *"Goddamnit!"*

The edge was back and Haskins' toes were over it. Both officers from team two called in Mr. Thummel's, a.k.a. Giggins', death into the station and requested assistance, knowing team three would also hear the news.

Meanwhile, Officer Haskins and his partner made their way over to the *gurney* under the stairs. *A gurney.* Of all things it could be, why had Haskins adopted that? Because that's what the blasted thing looked like. Makeshift, sure. A little unconventional—perhaps. Probably created for a battlefield or something. Maybe even space. Take the legs off and *voilà*—a floating gurney.

With every step Haskins took toward the gurney, the more he saw of a nude outline of a human underneath the ice.

"Goddamnit!" Angered, Sergeant Haskins turned his head away and pursed his lips; his feet taking him to where he didn't want to go but had to—it was his duty. Oh, how he wished God answered more prayer instead of damning everyone and everything.

"Damn it!" If he could burn this scenario in eternal flames like it never happened, he would. But that's not how the world works. And, apparently, God, too. When people wish something bad on someone, *damns* them, nothing ever happens, even when it's deserved. But, *oh*, when the almighty damns *you*—you're fucked. Not only in this life, but the next.

Over the chest, an apparatus pushed down into the ice and then raised. A pump, attached to the side of the gurney, breathed as it expanded and exhaled when it collapsed. A faint whistle of moving air sounded through tubes.

Taking a deep breath and saying a prayer, Sergeant Haskins reached into a pocket and snapped on a rubber glove, which had become standard issue nowadays, as law enforcement increasingly encountered more unknown substances than most scientists do in labs.

As he reached for the ice covering the head, that chest apparatus pushed again, startling him. Then, the pump breathed and exhaled. The body in the ice made him realize he could be in a worse state.

Gloved fingers carefully brushed the ice off the face as an archeologist would brush off a find. To his horror, the face: pale, cold, unmoving belonged to a young girl—Abbie.

Instead of looking away, Haskins' eyes soaked her in, engraving her in his mind; his partner stared, too. Not in some sick, perverted way, but as motivation. Another reminder of how he had gotten so damn tired of people's shit in the world that he vowed whomever and whatever he could stop, he would. It's a dirty, messy job, but someone had to slow the flow of shit before everyone drowned in it. It's why he became a cop.

But it's getting harder to wash off the smell—and control himself. The itch could be unbearable at times. There was no way he would or could discipline team two's leader for expending an extra shot. Doing so would muck-up a clear conscience. Especially when he wanted nothing more than to fire a machine gun at the turd, lying on the floor, until nothing—

"HA-AAAAAH!"

Ice rustled in the gurney; apparatuses detached from its side and fell to the dirt floor.

"Jesus Christ!" Haskins crapped out of his mouth; he and his partner backed away from the gurney; both officers of team two snapped their sight to under the stairs to see what the hell was happening.

All living eyes stared at Abbie, who sat upright in the gurney tub.

"Abbie? Abbie!?" sounded from the top of the stairs

by the basement door—a woman's voice. Then, the sound of footsteps coming down the basement steps. *"Abbie!?"*

"Who's that?" Haskins wanted to know.

His partner trotted to the bottom of the steps, looked up, looked at the Sergeant, and shrugged he didn't know.

"Abbie!? It's mom."

"Jesus! Stop her!" Sergeant Haskins barked.

His partner ascended only a few steps before meeting her. "Ma'am, please go back upstairs."

"Where's Abbie!? Where's my daughter!?" Mrs. Syfert cried.

"Let's go upstairs and we'll fill you in on everything."

Mrs. Syfert turned partially on the steps, so the officer grabbed her shoulders and turned her back.

"I demand to see my—"

Abbie's mother recognized Abbie's cell phone on top of a pile of muddied clothes lying beside the bottom of the steps.

"ABBIE! ABBIE!" she wailed, pushing the officer, trying to get downstairs; her face an instant mess, pale and wet.

During the commotion, the officer from team two calmly called into the station, requesting medical assistance for Abbie.

"ABBIE! Someone said, Abbie!" Mrs. Syfert groaned, pushing harder on the officer.

Pissed, Haskins turned, showing his teeth at the officer who called into the station.

"Yes, that's right. Same name," the officer communicated, unwilling to repeat the girl's name, knowing Haskins wasn't showing off his pearly whites.

If he said her name again, those choppers would be stained red after the Sergeant got done biting his head off.

"*NO! MOVE!* I got to see my daughter! " Mrs. Syfert pushed, but the officer wasn't budging. "Get out of the way! Why won't you let me see my daughter? *ABBIE!*"

Drained, the mother started to collapse, turning sideways on the stairs. The angle made it difficult for the officer to catch her, but he did, holding her upright with her bony shoulder in his chest and his hands interlocked around her outside shoulder. Through the openings between the wooden steps, she saw movement and commotion—then a glimpse of her daughter.

"*ABBIE!!! ABBIE!!!*" A flurry of adrenaline energized Abbie's mom.

"Calm down, ma'am."

"But that's Abbie! *Pleeeaaase!*"

Her body grew heavy in the officer's arms; the adrenaline waned faster than it had come.

"I…want…to…see…my…daugh…"

In the officer's arms, she fainted.

36

Eventually, Mrs. Syfert came to and saw her daughter—when she had identified the body.

The act never registered entirely—a nightmare more than a memory. More accurately, a memorable nightmare far removed from reality other than she had it. For she sat on her daughter's bed, waiting for Abbie to show up and surprise her. It all had to be a—

Her hand cupped a beer can. The beer smelled like warm piss and tasted as bad as it smelled she imagined. Her urine had smelled like that before—yeasty—when she hadn't drunk enough water. But it was the only drop of alcohol in the house. Whoever stamped the date on it smeared the damn thing, so it was anyone's guess how old it was. If she had to guess, she would say it was from her husband's last beer run.

She was never much of a drinker as an adult,

especially when she had learned she was pregnant with Abbie and had drunk little since, only on special occasions.

Now was one of those times. For soon, everyone would see that this whole thing had been a mistake: a ginormous botched misunderstanding and a premature verification of death. Any moment now, her baby would walk through that door and run up the steps to see her mama.

Until then, the pain! The goddamn pain!

Nightmares usually end, don't they? Even repetitive ones must give up after a while.

This one might not end. Daphne swore she had seen her daughter alive, sitting up in some portable hospital bed. She had to be alive, right, to be sitting up? In Daphne's world, the dead *don't* sit up. In the real world, of course, they can—and do. Some die sitting. And no matter how death comes, whether by nature, complications, being at the wrong place at the wrong time, one's own hand, or at the hand of another, it just happens. In viewing them from the back, it would be hard to tell the state of a person. Still, she wholeheartedly believed she had seen her daughter sitting up and alive.

That was right before she had passed out. What she had seen occurred between consciousness and unconsciousness and, as foggy as that transition was, she was still painfully aware of her surroundings. Her eyes and brain hadn't lied.

The authorities lied. When Daphne wanted an answer as to how it was possible her daughter was alive one minute only to wake up and find out her daughter was dead, the authorities told her Abbie had died *before* she saw her in the basement.

The dead don't sit up, Daphne couldn't shake out of her mind. Yet, the authorities had explained to her that the equipment, attached to the side of the gurney, was vital in keeping the body going. An oxygen machine, a resuscitation-like device, etcetera, had done just that: kept Abbie's body going.

Then, they went beyond that in momentarily reviving Abbie's body, and that was what Daphne had witnessed in the basement. As unfortunate and confusing as that was, that was all it was. About as uncertain as any death where there's not a body of proof. MIAs, POWs, any accident where the body, flesh and bone, had been incinerated without a trace. All hard-to-handle let alone hard-to-accept. Heavy shit for those left behind to carry it and, not to mention, stink to high heaven. And as she carried it, it was right under her nose.

Daphne had seen the body.

Surviving her daughter, she would serve the rest of her days in a concentration camp, about as impossible to break out of as being in a closed casket and buried six feet deep.

It wasn't impossible, of course. A few have escaped such camps. Many of whom would say in a lot of ways they're still trapped there. The experience still so fresh in their mind that they could visit anytime they choose to think about it.

Or, when it just popped up on its own.

We have all experienced this type of unwelcome intrusion. How or why the mind reminds without our command is anyone's guess. But it happens. And although Daphne, honestly, didn't want to entertain seeing her daughter sitting up in the gurney, it came way too often.

Perhaps, the mystery would not rest until it was solved. So, it went on living, visiting, and tormenting, like a ghost with unfinished business until the business was complete—the mystery solved.

The authorities knew this and tried to explain to Daphne what she felt was unexplainable. When the perpetrator was shot and killed, he was holding a needle containing a drug to prevent such momentary revitalization from happening, but he never had the chance to administer it. With Abbie's body under unbearable stress from the trauma she had experienced, they concluded her body had re-animated in a knee-jerk reaction and sat up. The medical examiner declared her legally dead from asphyxiation, logging an estimated time of death *prior* to her momentary resuscitation, believing that *'...the spirit God had breathed into Abbie at birth returned to him and she was absent from the body during those few moments of brief revival.'*

It all had to be a mistake. Daphne just hoped that her little girl hadn't been buried alive. For she would be as trapped as she was—in a casket buried six feet deep.

When she had asked the authorities as to why her daughter had been hooked up to those devices to keep her body going, they told her *'to be preserved.' 'Preserved for what?'* she had asked them. As much as they wanted to simplify it by using the analogy of buying meat at the supermarket, bringing it home, wrapping it, labeling it, and throwing it in the freezer to be eaten at a later date, they avoided the crude and insensitive by telling her the truth. And the truth was the perp was preparing Abbie for preservation, or what is called *cryonics*, to be re-animated at some point in the future when the methodology and technology were invented to do so.

This, of course, drove Daphne farther into the fog.

'Re-animated?' she had asked, and they had said, *'Yes, ma'am. To be brought back to life.'*

She couldn't believe what she was hearing. All of it was too impossible to believe. Preserving a body for a later time? Experience told her two times over: dead was dead. Her husband never came back and wasn't going to. Nor was Oliver.

But Abbie's situation would be different. Being told her daughter was dead wasn't enough for it to sink in or be accepted. *'...the spirit God had breathed into Abbie at birth returned to him and she was absent from the body during those few moments of brief revival,'* they had said.

How the hell do they know! Daphne protested in her mind. *Can they see spirits? Do they have a direct line with God?*

Who does? Daphne thought. *Maybe Abbie's spirit was still inside her. Yes, and that would bring her back. She came back once. Am I crazy? Holding out hope when I'm burying my daughter tomorrow.*

Where's God? Why does he allow these things to happen? Does he hate me? What did I do? In two years, I've lost everything!

In reliving the memory of telling Abbie she loved her one final time before getting into the *all-black* car—*black—car—black car—death—black death car*, the rhetoric in Daphne's mind silenced and all she could hear was her daughter saying, *'I love you, too, Mom.'*

"Aaaugh!" Daphne cried aloud.

A hand went over her constricting chest, unable to reach inside to her tightening heart. It felt as if the invisible God had reached inside her and imposed his will on the living to squeeze the life out of it. Her heart felt smaller. Every valve and chamber smooshed together and blocked.

In that smothering state, all of the parts of Abbie's life that Daphne had witnessed flashed across her mind. Her birth. Her first spoken word: *'Mom-my.'* Her first steps. Everything. Even things she had forgotten among the things she remembered all too well. Sobbing at her father's funeral, *'I love you, Dad.'* The anger after, *'It's not fair!'* On the couch crying over Oliver, *'There's just you and I left, Mom.'* Her naked body sitting upright in the gurney. Seeing her daughter, her only child, lying lifeless when she had ID'd the body—a young life cut way too short.

Mrs. Syfert knew she was dying on her daughter's bed. A heart attack, a stroke, or by God's hand, it didn't matter, because it was happening. In that suffocating, euphoric state, she re-experienced the wobbliness in her legs, the alcohol smell of a sterile room, and the surreal circumstance that had brought her to the morgue. A coroner, wearing rubber gloves, pulled down the sheet, revealing her daughter's face. *'Is this your daughter, ma'am?'*

The recollection occurred again, but this time differently. Alone in the sterile room, Daphne felt wobbly, looking at the sheet covering her daughter's body. Abruptly, Abbie sat up with the sheet over her head like a ghost, the fabric sucking into the mouth as she gasped for breath. When the material relaxed, the sheet rolled off her head and down her body, gathering at her waist. Mechanically, Abbie turned her dead, blue head and looked at her mom. Her six-year-old voice spoke out of her teen body, "I'm dead, Mommy. Sorry to leave you all by yourself. But I love you, Mommy."

"AAAAUUUGH…God!" Mrs. Syfert wailed as her heart tightened more.

Her baby will never have the chance to take a

chance. Get married. Have children. Travel. See her grandchildren. Grow old. For Abbie had skipped all of that and went straight to the dying part.

Raising her eyes toward the ceiling, seeing beyond, into heaven perhaps, she yelled, "Just do it!"

Calmer, wiping tears and holding a beer, she whispered, "Just do it."

Her heart felt like it was going to collapse at any moment. This gave her peace. Although it felt foreign, its serenity couldn't be mistaken. Strange how not having something for so long could feel right and sure.

What am I doing? In defiance, she shook her head harder than she ever had, nearly causing whiplash.

No! No! Abbie's at a friend's house doing homework or hanging out. Any minute she'll walk through that door, yelling to me she's home.

"I can't leave her alone."

For some reason, she had said that last part aloud.

"Hold on. *Just*—hold on."

Not everyone could, but Daphne had held on to hope so many times when there wasn't any that she became good at fooling herself there was some hope to hold on to when there wasn't. In tricking herself, she lived those years. Good or bad, she lived them. And her hope was added to every so many years. Her husband, then Abbie, had supplied real hope, tangible. And don't discount the dog.

Half of her hope instantly disappeared when her husband had died. A little more with Oliver. Not having any hope in herself, she still had hope in Abbie. Which, she held onto now, loosely.

'I'm dead, Mommy. Sorry to leave you all by yourself. But I love you, Mommy.'

"Abbie's dead," Mrs. Syfert whispered.

Rocking on the bed, she repeated, "Abbie's dead. Oh, no, Abbie's dead. Abbie's dead. Abbie's dead."

Daphne's eyes rolled to the back of her head. Everything she had acquired in life and stored in her brain decompartmentalized and jumbled together into an unorganized pile of knowledge and images. Her body stopped rocking and convulsed to an uneven rhythm; her heart skipped beats. Her fragile spirit grasped for hope and, if not hope, anything worth holding on to. Only life's cord dangled before her. She ignored it, looking for another, but there wasn't another, only life. Everything about her bent, on the verge of breaking, unable to carry the weight of her failing mental, emotional, physical, and spiritual state.

She was coming undone—a peeled, rotten banana.

And it stunk—right under her nose.

At the very last moment, Daphne grabbed life's cord and held on. It wasn't an umbilical cord, far from, for this cord wasn't about to provide anything more than more days. Needs and everything else would have to come by her own effort.

It's exhausting doing that, so she contemplated letting go.

"Why so cruel, God? Why?"

Ironically, Mrs. Thummel had asked the same question when she had thought her children had died in the car accident.

Then, a revelatory blank erased all that Mrs. Syfert was going through. The episode ended. With arms straight out in front of her, both of her hands grasped the beer can as if it were life's cord, beer spilling onto the comforter. Asking why this time, she knew why.

I cut out the ad. I handed it to her. 'Ya know, get your mind off things,' she had said to her daughter. *She doesn't have a mind. Not anymore.*

Feeling the can in her fingers, she imagined its metal slicing across her wrists.

I killed my daughter.

If I let go of the can does that mean I let go of life? I want...

Downstairs, the side door to the kitchen opened. No question, Daphne had lived there long enough to know. Acquired hearing from listening for Abbie when she had stayed out late with friends.

Listening, Daphne lowered the beer can and cleared her throat.

The door closed.

Setting the can on the nightstand, Daphne slid and sat on the edge of the bed, listening.

A drawer opened in the kitchen, then closed.

She slid off the bed and stood inside the bedroom doorway, leaning forward on stacked hands against its frame.

Another drawer opened, its contents noisily sifted through.

Filled with hope, Daphne moved into the hall to the top of the stairs. Hearing the drawer close, she scooted down the steps. "Abbie!? Abbie!? Is that you?"

Afterword

I may have gotten a few things wrong regarding cryonics, and my proposals may be horseshit. Still, if you enjoyed the story, then I accomplished what I had set out to do. I find cryonics interesting, the idea of freezing a dead body in hopes of resurrecting it in the future. Storing the corpse inside a tank is another way of burying the dead. Outside of this intrigue, I am indifferent to it—nothing more than a mere bystander, observing.

You might be asking, *Observing what?* The same as you, my friend—to see if it can be done.

If it can, nearly every can of worms humankind has placed on pantry shelves for a rainy day since our existence will open and spill out. It will be messy. For what man has conveniently packaged will empty. Not worms, either. No, I'm talking about things way more toxic—human things—such as questions, doubts, misunderstandings, and mysteries. They will spill onto the so-called foundations of science, theology, and morality and erode them, leaving many standing on new ground. Some will love it, and some will hate it. Undoubtedly, some remarkable things have happened during man's existence. But nothing will clear out the pantry faster than resurrecting, not resuscitating, a dead person. Cloning a human would equally mess up the pantry.

But don't worry. If cryonics ever succeeds, humans will re-stock the pantry to the gills. Organized in a way that will suggest humans understand once more.

With that said, I don't care if cryonics succeeds or fails. Nor will you find me discriminate one way or the other. To each their own.

In this spirit, I recorded this fictional story as it unfolded within me without any intentional lean on my part. I cannot be any clearer.

W. G. TUTTLE

November 3, 2016

ABOUT **THE AUTHOR**

W. G. TUTTLE is an American writer of riveting science fiction, thriller, and suspense novels and short stories. He is the author of the novels Try To Sleep, Those Who Long, October Midnight, and War For The Spheres. He has also written numerous short stories, including Scranton October 1894, Vacation's End, Where Did THEY Come From?, and Standard Issue Spirits.

He also writes screenplays and intelligent non-fiction about stocks, investing, and trading.

Born: January 27, 1972, Binghamton, New York

Full name: Walter George Tuttle, Jr.

Spouse: Shawn M. Tuttle (m.1997)

Children: 1 son & 1 daughter

Alma mater: The Pennsylvania State University

Influenced by: Frank Herbert, H. G. Wells, Ramsey Campbell (Carl Dreadstone), Arthur C. Clarke, Isaac Asimov, Stanislaw Lem, William Peter Blatty, Ira Levin, Robert Bloch, Ian Fleming, Alistair MacLean

wgtuttle.com